Dragon Romance: Hearts of Ice

Michael Schuerman

Published by Fandom Books 2024

While every precaution has been taken in the preparation of this book, the publisher assumes no responsibility for error or omissions, or for damages resulting from the use of the information contained herein.

Dragon Romance: Hearts of Ice

First Edition. October 24, 2024

Copywrite © 2024 Fandom Books

Written by Michael Schuerman.

Contents

The Ice Queen's Domain 4

The Dragon Slayer's Mission 10

The Frozen Forest 16

The First Encounter 28

A Queen's Challenge 43

The Dragon's Curse 57

A Dance of Fire and Ice 65

The Hunter and the Hunted 73

Cracks in the Ice 81

A Night of Secrets 92

The Heart of the Ice Dragon 99

The Attack 107

The Fire Within 113

The Thawing Heart 119

The Ice Queen's Dilemma 127

A Dragon's Choice 133

A Love Tested by Fire 140

The Betrayal Revealed 148

Hearts of Ice, Hearts of Fire 156

The Ice Queen's Domain

The wind howled through the towering peaks of the northern mountains, its icy tendrils wrapping around the jagged cliffs and sending flurries of snow spiraling into the sky. The kingdom of Soltara was a vast expanse of frozen wilderness, its forests blanketed in white, its rivers frozen solid beneath layers of thick ice. At the heart of this cold, forbidding land stood the Palace of Ice, a fortress carved from ancient glaciers, glittering like crystal in the weak northern sun.

And within its walls ruled the Ice Queen.

Esmeray stood at the edge of her balcony, gazing out over her kingdom, her breath visible in the freezing air. The morning light touched her pale skin, her dark hair swirling in the frigid wind. From a distance, she might have looked like a statue—still, regal, unmovable. Her expression was one of cold indifference, her eyes the color of ice, piercing and unreadable.

The transformation would come soon. She could feel it stirring within her, the shift from woman to dragon—a curse she had lived with for centuries. By day, she would rule her kingdom as the mighty ice dragon, her scales as white as snow, her breath capable of freezing anything in its path. By night, she returned to her human form, though her heart remained as frozen as the landscape she governed.

Esmeray's fingers brushed the cold stone railing of her balcony, her thoughts distant. The sky above was a pale gray, heavy with the promise of more snow, but her mind was elsewhere, far from the kingdom she had ruled with an iron grip for so long. She had known solitude for centuries, had embraced it. Love, she had learned, was a weakness—a vulnerability she could no longer afford.

Her heart, once warm, had been turned to ice, locked away behind walls so thick not even the fiercest fire could melt them.

As the first stirrings of the curse began to ripple through her body, Esmeray turned away from the view. She moved with grace and precision, every step purposeful as she crossed the vast hall of her palace, her gown trailing behind her like a shadow. Her footsteps echoed in the empty space, the sound swallowed by the cold, lifeless air.

A servant, a young man with trembling hands, appeared at the doorway, bowing low as she approached. "Your Majesty," he stammered, his voice shaking as much from fear as from the cold. "The council has assembled as you requested."

Esmeray barely glanced at him, her gaze as sharp as the frost that covered the palace walls. "I will join them shortly," she said, her voice like the crack of ice breaking across a frozen lake. Dismissed, the servant scurried away, his footsteps hurried as if he couldn't escape fast enough.

Esmeray didn't blame him. Most of her subjects feared her, and that was how she preferred it. Fear kept them obedient, kept them in line. She ruled Soltara with a firm hand, her dragons patrolling the skies, ensuring that no one dared defy her. And in return, her people lived in peace, untouched by the wars and turmoil that plagued the lands to the south.

Peace, she thought bitterly. It came at a price.

The curse was both her punishment and her power. By day, she was a dragon, her heart encased in ice, her soul bound to the cold. By night, she became human again, but the warmth of love and connection had long since been stripped from her. She had accepted this fate centuries ago, had convinced herself that power was the only thing that mattered.

Love was for fools. And she was no fool.

With a final glance at the fading sunlight outside, Esmeray moved toward the council chamber. The hallways were silent as always, her servants knowing better than to disturb their queen without reason. The doors to the chamber were tall and heavy, carved from ancient ice, and they swung open with barely a sound as she approached.

Inside, the council members—a group of advisors, generals, and dragon commanders—stood at attention. Their faces were as cold and rigid as the ice walls that surrounded them, their gazes lowering as Esmeray entered the room.

"Your Majesty," one of the advisors, an older man with white hair and a lined face, spoke as she took her place at the head of the table. "We have received troubling reports from the southern borders. It seems the southern king is planning a move against us. There are rumors that he has hired a dragon slayer."

Esmeray's eyes narrowed at the mention of a dragon slayer. It wasn't the first time someone had tried to take her throne, but dragon slayers were rare and dangerous. She had faced them before, but none had ever come close to challenging her.

"Let him come," Esmeray said, her voice low and dangerous. "He will meet the same fate as the others."

The advisor shifted nervously, clearly hesitant to speak further. "This one is different, Your Majesty. His name is Darian. He has slain more dragons than any of his kind. He is… formidable."

Esmeray's lips curved into a cold smile. "I will deal with this Darian myself."

The council members exchanged uneasy glances, but no one dared to object. Esmeray's reputation as a ruthless ruler was well known, and none of them were foolish enough to question her judgment. She had ruled for centuries, her power unmatched, her dragons loyal to her command.

"I will await his arrival," Esmeray continued, her gaze turning toward the window, where the sky had begun to darken. "And when he comes, he will understand why the Ice Queen's heart cannot be melted."

The room was silent, the weight of her words settling over the council like a layer of frost. Esmeray stood, the beginnings of her transformation stirring once more within her. Soon, she would be the dragon again, the powerful creature that had kept her kingdom in line for so long.

As she left the chamber and made her way back toward her private quarters, Esmeray's thoughts drifted to the dragon slayer. She had no doubt that he would come—foolish humans always did. They thought they could defeat her, that they could end her reign and claim her power. But Esmeray was different. She was not like the other dragons, the ones who fell to the blades of men like Darian.

She was cursed, yes. But her curse made her strong.

As the transformation began in earnest, Esmeray felt the familiar rush of power, her skin growing colder, her bones lengthening, her senses sharpening. In moments, she would be a dragon, her wings spread wide, her breath capable of freezing anything in its path.

But even in her dragon form, even as she embraced the strength that came with the curse, there was a small, distant part of her—a part she rarely allowed herself to acknowledge—that felt the ache of loneliness. It was a feeling she had long since buried, a feeling she had taught herself to ignore.

Love was weakness. And she would never be weak again.

As the final stages of the transformation took hold, Esmeray let out a roar that echoed through the mountains, a sound that sent shivers down the spines of those who heard it. She was the Ice Queen, ruler of the north, and no one—least of all a dragon slayer—would ever break through the walls she had built around her heart.

The Dragon Slayer's Mission

The southern sun hung high in the sky, casting a golden glow over the grand city of Eldoria. Its bustling streets were filled with merchants, travelers, and nobles, but all the activity seemed distant and irrelevant to Darian as he stood in the throne room of the king. The walls of the chamber were lined with towering columns and tapestries, but Darian's sharp green eyes were fixed solely on the man before him—the king of the southern lands, who sat upon his gilded throne with a look of grave determination.

"Your Majesty," Darian said, his voice steady as he bowed low. "I came as soon as I received your summons."

King Alaric, a broad-shouldered man with silver in his hair and a crown that gleamed in the sunlight streaming through the windows, nodded. "I'm glad to see you, Darian. You've proven yourself many times over as the greatest dragon slayer in the realm. I have a task for you… one that only you can accomplish."

Darian straightened, his expression calm but curious. He had been called upon by kings and queens before, each of them asking him to rid their lands of dragons—creatures he had spent his entire life hunting and killing. But there was something different about the way King Alaric spoke, a weight in his voice that suggested this mission was unlike any other.

"I'm ready to serve, Your Majesty," Darian said confidently. "What is it you require?"

King Alaric's gaze darkened as he rose from his throne, his heavy cloak sweeping behind him as he stepped toward Darian. "The northern lands are ruled by the Ice Queen, Esmeray," he began, his voice low. "For centuries, she has kept her kingdom isolated, but that is beginning to change. Her dragons have been seen venturing farther south, threatening our borders, burning villages and freezing entire armies. The Ice Queen's power is growing, and if we do not stop her soon, she will sweep down upon the south with the full force of her dragons."

Darian's brow furrowed, his hand instinctively resting on the hilt of his sword. He had heard rumors of the Ice Queen, tales of a dragon ruler in the far north who commanded an army of ice-breathing beasts. But he had never paid them much mind—until now.

"You want me to kill her," Darian said, his voice steady. It wasn't a question, but a statement of fact. He had been a dragon slayer for most of his life, hunting down the dangerous creatures that terrorized the lands. This mission, though daunting, felt like just another challenge—another dragon to slay.

King Alaric nodded, his face grim. "Yes. But be warned, Darian. This is no ordinary dragon. Esmeray is unlike any creature you've ever faced. She is cursed to live as a dragon by day and a woman by night, but whether in human or dragon form, she is dangerous beyond measure. Her magic is strong, her heart cold. If you are to succeed, you must strike swiftly and without mercy."

Darian's eyes flickered with interest. A dragon queen who could shift between forms? He had faced powerful dragons before, but this sounded different, more complex. Still, he was confident in his abilities. He had slain the fiercest of beasts, and this one—no matter her curse—would fall like the rest.

"I will travel to the north and end her reign," Darian said, his voice resolute. "Her dragons will no longer threaten the south."

King Alaric looked at him for a long moment, his expression unreadable. "I trust you will not fail me, Darian. The safety of my people depends on it."

Darian nodded firmly, and with that, the king dismissed him. He turned and walked out of the grand throne room, his mind already on the journey ahead. As he passed through the palace corridors, he felt a surge of excitement rise in his chest. It had been months since he had taken on a mission of this magnitude, and though the Ice Queen was said to be powerful, Darian welcomed the challenge.

Outside, the palace courtyard was bathed in the warm light of the southern sun, a stark contrast to the icy lands that awaited him in the north. His horse, a powerful black stallion, waited for him at the gates, saddled and ready for the long journey ahead.

"You're about to see snow for the first time, my friend," Darian muttered as he stroked the horse's mane, a small smile playing on his lips.

He mounted the horse with practiced ease, glancing back at the palace one last time before turning toward the distant mountains. The road north was long and treacherous, but he had faced worse. He knew the stories of the frozen wilderness, the dangers of the northern dragons and the bitter cold, but nothing would stop him from completing his mission.

As he urged his horse forward, Darian's mind wandered back to what the king had said about Esmeray—how she transformed from dragon to human, cursed to live in both worlds. He had never encountered such a creature before, and a part of him was curious. What kind of woman could rule an entire kingdom of dragons with an iron fist? How had she come to be cursed?

"Best not to wonder too much," Darian muttered to himself. "She's a dragon, and a dangerous one at that. Don't lose focus."

He had learned long ago that getting emotionally involved in his missions was a sure way to fail. Dragons were beasts, and though they were intelligent, they were still enemies to humankind. He had spent years perfecting the art of killing them, and this would be no different.

Yet, as the miles passed and the warmth of the southern lands gave way to the biting cold of the north, Darian couldn't help but wonder about the woman behind the curse. Was she truly as cold and heartless as the stories claimed? Or was there something more behind the legend?

By the time the sun began to set, casting a pale orange light over the snowy landscape, Darian had reached the edge of the frozen forests that marked the beginning of Esmeray's domain. The temperature had dropped significantly, the air cold enough to sting his skin, but Darian was prepared. He had donned his thickest furs, his sword strapped securely to his side, his mind focused on the task ahead.

The journey would be dangerous. The Ice Queen's dragons patrolled these lands, and they would not take kindly to an outsider. But Darian had fought dragons before, and he knew how to stay hidden, how to strike without warning. He would bide his time, study the queen and her dragons, and when the moment was right, he would strike.

As he rode deeper into the frozen wilderness, the sky darkened, and the wind picked up, howling through the trees like the mournful cries of spirits. Darian kept his head down, his eyes scanning the horizon for any sign of movement. The northern lands were desolate and unforgiving, but Darian had faced worse and come out victorious.

He had no doubt that he would face the Ice Queen and defeat her, just as he had defeated every dragon that had crossed his path. Yet, as the night grew colder and the silence of the north enveloped him, Darian couldn't shake the strange feeling that this mission was different—that Esmeray was different.

But for now, all he had was the road ahead, the cold wind at his back, and the certainty that he would not fail.

For he was Darian, the greatest dragon slayer in the realm, and nothing—not even the Ice Queen—could stop him.

The Frozen Forest

The sun had long since disappeared beneath the horizon, leaving the northern sky bathed in a faint twilight glow. The cold air nipped at Darian's face, each breath forming a cloud of mist as he urged his horse deeper into the Frozen Forest. Towering trees, their branches heavy with snow, surrounded him on all sides, casting long shadows across the narrow path. The world around him felt eerily quiet, save for the occasional creak of ice shifting beneath the weight of the frost.

Darian gripped the reins of his horse tightly, his eyes scanning the landscape for any sign of movement. He had heard the stories—the Frozen Forest was not a place for the faint of heart. It was said to be home to creatures twisted by the magic of the Ice Queen, beasts with frost in their veins and death in their eyes. Frost-breathing wolves, ice serpents, and worse stalked these woods, waiting for travelers who dared to venture too far into the north.

"Keep steady," Darian muttered to his horse, patting its neck reassuringly. The animal's breath came in short, nervous puffs, its ears flicking back and forth at every sound. Darian could feel the tension in the air, the oppressive weight of the forest pressing down on them. It was as if the very trees were watching him, waiting for something to happen.

The path ahead wound deeper into the heart of the forest, the snow growing thicker with every step. Darian's mind wandered back to the stories he had heard about the Ice Queen, Esmeray. A ruler so powerful and feared, even the elements seemed to bow to her will. It was said that she could summon storms with a mere thought, freeze armies with a single breath. And then there was the curse—a tale whispered in hushed voices by those who dared to speak of it.

The curse that bound her to live as a dragon by day, and a woman by night.

Darian had always dismissed such stories as mere legend. But the deeper he traveled into the north, the more he began to wonder if there was some truth to them. The air itself seemed alive with magic, crackling with an energy that made the hair on the back of his neck stand on end.

He had faced dragons before—ferocious creatures with fire and fury in their hearts. But this was different. Esmeray was different. She wasn't just a dragon. She was a ruler, a queen, and her power extended far beyond the physical realm. The very thought of confronting her stirred something deep within him, something more than just the thrill of the hunt.

Darian shook his head, forcing himself to focus. "Stay sharp," he whispered to himself, tightening his grip on the reins. "She's still a dragon. Just another mission."

Suddenly, a low growl echoed through the trees, sending a chill down Darian's spine. His horse jerked beneath him, its eyes wide with fear as it pranced nervously in place.

"What is it?" Darian muttered, instinctively reaching for the sword at his side.

Before he could react, a shadow darted between the trees ahead, moving with an eerie grace. Another growl followed, this time closer, and Darian's heart began to race. His hand tightened around the hilt of his sword as his eyes scanned the forest, searching for the source of the sound.

Out of the corner of his eye, he saw it—a pair of glowing blue eyes staring at him from the darkness. Then another. And another. The wolves had found him.

A pack of frost-breathing wolves, their fur as white as the snow beneath their feet, emerged from the shadows, their breath visible in the cold air as they circled him. Their eyes gleamed with hunger, their lips curling back to reveal sharp, gleaming teeth. These were no ordinary wolves. The Ice Queen's magic had twisted them into something far more dangerous.

Darian's horse reared in panic, its hooves striking the air as it tried to bolt. But Darian held firm, pulling the reins sharply and steadying the animal. He knew that running would only make things worse. The wolves were faster, more cunning. He had to face them.

Drawing his sword in one fluid motion, Darian slid off his horse, keeping his eyes locked on the wolves. His breath came in short, controlled bursts as he assessed the situation. There were at least six of them, maybe more hiding in the shadows. They moved in perfect sync, their movements slow and deliberate as they closed in around him.

"Come on, then," Darian muttered under his breath, his muscles coiled and ready. "Let's get this over with."

The lead wolf, its eyes blazing with an almost unnatural light, crouched low, its gaze locked on Darian with deadly intent. The growl that rumbled from its chest was deep and menacing, a promise of the violence to come. Without warning, it sprang forward, claws extended, mouth open wide as it aimed for Darian's throat.

Darian, with instincts honed over years of battles, sidestepped the wolf's attack just in time. His sword flashed in the pale, dim light of the forest as he swung out, his blade cutting deep into the wolf's side. The wolf let out a pained, guttural yelp, stumbling and collapsing into the snow, but Darian had no time to revel in his victory. Another wolf was on him in an instant, lunging from his left, its sharp teeth snapping perilously close to his forearm.

Gritting his teeth, Darian twisted his body, bringing his sword down in a swift, deadly arc. The blade met the wolf's neck with a sickening crunch, sending it to the ground in a lifeless heap. But even as it fell, Darian's eyes scanned the shifting shadows around him, where more wolves emerged, their blue eyes glowing like tiny shards of ice in the darkness.

He barely had a moment to catch his breath before the wolves closed in, their movements synchronized, silent as they advanced. They were relentless, their jaws snapping and claws slashing, their icy breath filling the air around him. They darted in and out of the shadows, each wolf waiting for an opening, an opportunity to strike. Darian had seen animals hunt in packs before, but never like this. These wolves were like shadows of each other, each one moving in perfect coordination with the others, as if driven by a single mind.

Darian's sword was a blur, cutting through the air with deadly precision. His every move was calculated, his body shifting and pivoting as he fought to keep the wolves at bay. He swung his blade, feeling the jarring impact each time it connected with flesh and bone. Yet with each wolf he struck down, another would leap to take its place, snarling and snapping with renewed ferocity.

The bitter cold began to seep into his bones, slowing his movements just enough to give the wolves an advantage. The snow beneath his boots was slick with blood, and every breath he took felt like shards of glass piercing his lungs. Despite the chill, sweat poured down his face, and he could feel his muscles tiring under the unyielding onslaught. The wolves were relentless, driven by a force he could almost feel pressing down on him—the chilling touch of the Ice Queen's magic, wrapping around him like an invisible web.

Two wolves lunged at him simultaneously, one from the front and the other from behind. Darian spun, parrying the first with a swift upward stroke before thrusting his blade back to catch the second wolf in the chest. The creature yelped, falling back into the snow, but as soon as it dropped, three more closed in, their icy breath filling the air around him, visible even in the faint light. They growled in unison, forming a tight circle, their eyes locked on him with an unsettling intelligence.

With his sword raised, Darian took a step back, his heart racing as he prepared for the next attack. But this time, the wolves didn't charge. Instead, they prowled around him in a tight circle, their growls echoing through the trees. The leader of the pack, a massive wolf with patches of frost clinging to its white fur, bared its teeth, its glowing blue eyes fixed on Darian with something almost like recognition. It let out a long, low howl, and the other wolves responded, the haunting sound filling the frozen forest.

Darian's grip tightened on his sword, his pulse pounding in his ears as he met the alpha wolf's gaze. For a moment, he could swear he saw something familiar in those icy eyes—a flicker of understanding, perhaps even intelligence. But he didn't have time to wonder. The wolves lunged again, and this time, they attacked in pairs, their movements so perfectly synchronized that it felt as if they were operating as one creature.

He swung his blade in wide arcs, trying to keep them at a distance, but the wolves were quick, their claws scraping against his armor, their teeth snapping inches from his flesh. One wolf sank its teeth into his boot, and he kicked out with all his strength, sending it sprawling back into the snow. Another leaped at him from the side, its claws digging into his shoulder, but he twisted, driving his sword into its chest.

The fight blurred into a frenzy of movement, his sword flashing as he struck again and again, his breaths coming in ragged gasps. His arms ached, his muscles burning with exhaustion, but he refused to falter. He knew that if he let his guard down for even a moment, the wolves would overwhelm him.

As he fought, the stories he'd heard from the villagers came rushing back to him—the tales of how the Ice Queen's magic seeped into the land, twisting everything it touched. These wolves weren't just animals. They were part of her magic, loyal to her will, and they would fight to the death to protect her domain.

A flash of movement caught his eye, and he turned just in time to see the alpha wolf charging at him, its massive form barreling through the snow with terrifying speed. Darian braced himself, his sword raised as the wolf leaped, its powerful jaws snapping inches from his face. He swung his blade in a desperate arc, feeling the impact as the blade connected with the wolf's shoulder. The creature howled in pain, but its momentum carried it forward, knocking Darian to the ground.

Snow filled his mouth and nose as he hit the ground, his vision blurring as he struggled to breathe. The wolf was on top of him, its jaws snapping dangerously close to his throat, its icy breath chilling his skin. Darian's hands scrambled for his sword, his fingers closing around the hilt just as the wolf lunged forward, teeth bared.

With a surge of strength, Darian drove the sword upward, feeling the blade sink into the wolf's chest. The creature let out a final, shuddering howl before collapsing on top of him, its body heavy and lifeless. Darian shoved it off, gasping for breath as he staggered to his feet, his vision spinning.

Only one wolf remained, circling him with a low growl. Darian steadied himself, raising his sword, ready for the final attack. But this wolf, smaller than the others, paused, its icy blue eyes meeting his with a glimmer of… hesitation?

Darian's heart pounded as he watched the creature, his sword poised to strike. But instead of attacking, the wolf let out a soft whine, its gaze lingering on him for a moment before it turned and disappeared into the shadows, its form melting into the trees as if it had never been there.

The forest was silent once more.

Darian stood there, his chest heaving as he took in his surroundings. Blood stained the snow around him, and the bodies of the fallen wolves lay scattered across the clearing, their once-fierce forms now still and lifeless. The cold bit into his skin, and the exhaustion weighed heavily on him, but he was alive.

He sheathed his sword, his hand still trembling from the intensity of the fight. As he caught his breath, his gaze drifted to the path ahead, where the shadows of the forest loomed, darker and more foreboding than ever. The Ice Queen's castle lay somewhere beyond those trees, waiting for him. And as he looked out into the darkness, he couldn't shake the feeling that this encounter had only been the beginning.

"Esmeray," he muttered under his breath, her name leaving his lips like a challenge.

The stories he'd heard, the legends of her power—they no longer felt like mere tales. He had seen her influence, felt the strength of her magic in the wolves that had fought so fiercely to protect her realm. But he wouldn't let that stop him.

Squaring his shoulders, Darian took a step forward, leaving the fallen wolves behind his mission was clear, but a question lingered at the back of his mind, haunting him as he pressed on.

Who was the Ice Queen, really? And why did he feel as though this battle had bound him to her in a way he couldn't yet understand?

As he walked, the shadows deepened, and the frozen wilderness seemed to close in around him, silent, watchful, and waiting.

The forest was silent once more.

For a moment, Darian allowed himself to catch his breath, his heart pounding in his chest. The wolves were dead, but the encounter had shaken him more than he cared to admit. He had fought dragons, beasts of unimaginable power, but this... this was different. The wolves were just a taste of what awaited him in the Ice Queen's domain.

He paused for a second as he wiped the blood from his sword and sheathed it, Darian glanced around, his senses heightened. The Ice Queen was near. He could feel it in the air, in the way the trees seemed to shiver with every gust of wind, in the way the cold seemed to cling to his skin.

He had to be close to her castle now. The Frozen Forest couldn't stretch much farther. But as he looked ahead, a sense of unease settled over him. The stories of Esmeray's power, her curse, played in the back of his mind. She wasn't just a dragon. She was something more—something far more dangerous than any creature he had faced before.

Darian mounted his horse once again, the animal's nervous energy still palpable. "Easy now," he murmured, patting its neck. "We're almost there."

As he rode deeper into the forest, the wind picked up, carrying with it the faint sound of a distant roar—a dragon's cry, echoing through the mountains.

Darian's jaw tightened, his hand instinctively going to the hilt of his sword. He was ready. Or at least, he told himself he was.

But as he neared the Ice Queen's castle, the weight of the mission pressed down on him like never before. He had slain dragons. He had fought beasts and monsters that haunted the darkest corners of the world.

But none of them had been Esmeray.

And none of them had made him question what he was truly walking into.

The First Encounter

The Ice Queen's palace loomed ahead, a vast fortress of glistening ice and intricate towers that spiraled toward the dark, northern sky. The structure shimmered in the moonlight, casting eerie reflections across the snowy ground, and Darian could hardly believe what he was seeing. The stories of her palace hadn't done it justice. Every tower, every arch seemed alive with a cold, unfeeling magic, as though the very walls held centuries of secrets.

Darian's grip tightened on his sword as he approached the main gate, his heart pounding in his chest. He was ready to face a dragon—ready for a battle against the creature that ruled this desolate land. His every instinct screamed at him to turn back, to flee the oppressive chill that seemed to emanate from the palace itself, but he ignored the voice of fear.

He had come too far to back down now.

The courtyard was empty, blanketed in a thick layer of untouched snow. It was as silent as death, with only the occasional whisper of wind slicing through the air. Darian's boots crunched softly in the snow as he advanced, his gaze darting to every shadow, every glimmer of movement.

The silence was broken by a low rumbling that sent a shiver down his spine. He looked up, his heart racing as a massive shape shifted atop one of the tallest towers. Moonlight glinted off scales as white as freshly fallen snow, and Darian's breath caught as he realized he was staring at the legendary Ice Queen in her dragon form.

Esmeray was beautiful and terrifying. Her scales shimmered with a crystalline glow, and her wings stretched wide, casting an enormous shadow over the courtyard below. Her eyes, a piercing blue, locked onto him, cold and calculating. She let out a low growl, the sound vibrating through the ground, as if warning him of the danger he faced.

Darian raised his sword, his muscles coiled, every nerve alive with anticipation. "I am here to end your reign, Ice Queen!" he shouted, his voice echoing against the palace walls. "You have terrorized these lands long enough."

The dragon's eyes narrowed, and for a brief, disorienting moment, Darian thought he saw a flicker of something—amusement, perhaps? She tilted her head slightly, watching him, and instead of attacking, she merely observed him, almost as though she were studying a curious creature.

Darian gritted his teeth, his heart hammering as he prepared to lunge. But before he could make a move, the dragon's massive form began to shimmer, shifting and twisting until, with a final burst of light, she was gone.

In her place stood a woman, tall and regal, her bearing as cold and unyielding as the ice that surrounded her. She wore a gown of shimmering silver, her hair as dark as midnight, cascading over her shoulders. Her pale skin seemed to glow in the moonlight, and her eyes—those same piercing blue eyes that had belonged to the dragon—were fixed on him with a mixture of disdain and curiosity.

Darian's breath caught, his mind reeling. He hadn't expected this. The legends spoke of her curse, yes, but seeing her transform from dragon to human was something else entirely. She was breathtaking, her beauty as fierce and unapproachable as a storm in winter.

Esmeray's lips curved into a slight, mocking smile as she took a step forward, her gaze never leaving his. "So," she said, her voice as cold and sharp as the air, "you're the dragon slayer they've sent to kill me."

Darian lowered his sword slightly, trying to mask his surprise. He'd expected a beast, a monster, but this woman... she was something else entirely. His resolve wavered, and he fought to steady himself, reminding himself of why he was here.

"Your reign has caused enough suffering," he said, his voice steady. "Your dragons have terrorized the southern lands, and it's time for that to end."

Esmeray laughed softly, the sound low and bitter, sending a chill down his spine. "Suffering?" she repeated, tilting her head as she studied him. "And you think you, a mortal man, can bring an end to it?"

Darian felt his frustration flare. She was mocking him, dismissing him as if he were nothing more than an insect. He straightened, his gaze hardening as he met her icy stare. "I've faced dragons before, Ice Queen," he said. "You're no different."

Esmeray's expression darkened, her eyes narrowing. "Is that so?" She took another step toward him, her presence both alluring and dangerous. "You speak of dragons as if they are mindless beasts. But you, dragon slayer, know nothing of what it is to rule."

Darian's jaw clenched. "I know enough to see that you're a tyrant."

Esmeray's gaze hardened, her voice turning to ice. "Do not presume to understand me, mortal. You know nothing of why I rule, or the price I've paid to do so."

For a moment, they stood in tense silence, their eyes locked. Darian's heart pounded, his mind racing as he tried to make sense of the emotions warring within him. He hadn't expected her to be so… human, so fierce and filled with emotion. And though he hated to admit it, there was something about her that intrigued him, something that made it difficult to see her as just another enemy.

Esmeray seemed to sense his hesitation, her gaze flickering with a glint of satisfaction. She took a step closer, her eyes gleaming. "You think yourself a hero, don't you?" she murmured, her voice soft, almost hypnotic. "A brave dragon slayer, here to vanquish the wicked queen."

Darian's breath caught, his hand tightening on the hilt of his sword as her words washed over him. He could feel the power radiating from her, the magnetic pull that seemed to draw him closer, despite his better judgment.

"I came here to end your tyranny," he said, his voice low. "To protect my people."

Esmeray's lips curved into a faint smile, one that didn't reach her eyes. "Your people." She took another step forward, close enough that he could feel the chill radiating from her skin. "And do your people care for you, dragon slayer? Do they mourn your absence?"

Darian felt a pang at her words, memories of his past, of battles fought and loved ones lost, surfacing unbidden. He shoved the thoughts aside, focusing on the woman before him, the queen who stood as his enemy.

"That's none of your concern," he said, his voice harsh. But the tremor in his tone betrayed him, and he saw the flicker of understanding in her eyes.

Esmeray's expression softened, if only for a moment, a brief flicker of vulnerability that surprised him. But just as quickly, it vanished, replaced by her usual icy mask. "You speak of ending my reign as if it were a simple matter," she said, her voice cool and measured. "But I am bound to this land, to the magic that flows through it. My kingdom is as much a part of me as my own flesh. You cannot kill one without killing the other."

Darian hesitated, his resolve wavering as her words sank in. He hadn't expected her to speak so openly, so honestly. He had come here to kill a monster, yet the woman before him was more complex, more human than he could have imagined.

But he couldn't afford to let his emotions cloud his judgment. He was here to complete a mission, to bring an end to the threat she posed to the southern lands.

Darian tightened his grip on his sword, raising it slightly as he squared his shoulders. "You may hide behind your magic, but that won't stop me," he said, his voice firm. "I will do whatever it takes to protect my people. Even if it means killing you."

Esmeray's gaze turned icy, her lips curving into a bitter smile. "Then you are a fool, dragon slayer," she said softly. "A fool who knows nothing of what it is to truly sacrifice."

Before he could respond, she stepped back, her figure blurring as the air around her shimmered with magic. In a flash of icy light, she was gone, leaving him standing alone in the courtyard, his heart racing, his mind a whirlwind of confusion.

Darian stared at the spot where she had stood, his mind struggling to process what had just happened. His heart pounded, his resolve wavering as he recalled the look in her eyes, the intensity of her gaze, the unspoken emotions that had flickered across her face.

This mission was different. She was different.

And as he stood there, alone in the shadow of her palace, he couldn't shake the feeling that this encounter was only the beginning—that Esmeray was more than just a monster, more than just a dragon queen.

But that didn't change his mission. He had a duty to fulfill, a people to protect. Yet, as he turned to leave the courtyard, the memory of her icy blue eyes lingered in his mind, a haunting reminder of the woman hidden behind the dragon.

The Ice Queen. Esmeray.

And for the first time, Darian found himself wondering if he truly had the strength to end her reign—or if he even wanted to.

As Darian stood in the courtyard, his mind spinning from his encounter with Esmeray, the silence was broken by a new presence. From the shadows of the palace gate, a figure emerged, cloaked in deep blue furs trimmed with silver, his dark hair brushed with streaks of frost. His expression was unreadable, his eyes a muted blue, lacking the piercing intensity of Esmeray's but carrying a quiet authority. He moved with a controlled, calculated grace, his gaze resting on Darian with something close to amusement.

"I see our queen has already left quite an impression," the man said, his voice smooth, almost mocking. He raised an eyebrow as he looked Darian up and down, noting the dragon slayer's slightly shaken stance. "Few make it this far into her domain. Even fewer leave in one piece."

Darian stiffened, his grip on his sword tightening instinctively as he sized up the stranger. "And who are you?" he asked warily.

The man let out a low chuckle. "Ah, forgive my lack of introduction," he said, inclining his head with a hint of mock politeness. "I am Thorian, advisor to Queen Esmeray, though some might say I am more of a… confidant." He paused, his eyes gleaming with something mischievous. "And occasionally, her conscience, though she rarely listens."

Darian scowled, unamused by Thorian's smug demeanor. He had dealt with plenty of advisors and nobles with that same arrogant air, men who thought themselves untouchable due to their proximity to power. But something about Thorian seemed different, as if he were more than just an advisor—a silent force operating within the palace, perhaps even keeping Esmeray's darker impulses in check.

"Her conscience," Darian repeated, a wry edge to his voice. "Then maybe you can tell me why a queen of dragons needs a conscience in the first place. Isn't she supposed to be ruthless?"

Thorian's eyes flickered with a strange, fleeting sadness. "Ruthless, yes. But ruthlessness comes at a price. A queen must be willing to sacrifice everything, even her own heart." He paused, his gaze growing more intense. "Something Esmeray knows all too well."

Darian's resolve wavered at Thorian's words. There was a weight behind them that suggested the advisor knew far more about Esmeray's past than he was letting on. But he forced himself to shake off the feeling, reminding himself of his mission.

"I didn't come here to understand her," Darian said, his tone hardening. "I came here to end her tyranny."

Thorian's lips curved into a faint smile, his gaze turning contemplative. "And yet, here you are, having faced her in her full dragon form, and still, you hesitate."

Darian's heart clenched at the truth behind the words. He hadn't expected Esmeray to be so... captivating. The shift from dragon to woman had caught him off guard, unraveling the simple hatred he'd expected to feel. Instead, he found himself filled with confusion, a strange pull he couldn't quite shake.

"Maybe I'm just waiting for the right moment," Darian replied defensively.

Thorian chuckled again, but there was no mirth in it. "Perhaps, or perhaps you're beginning to see that there is more to Esmeray than the Ice Queen's legend." He took a step closer, his gaze piercing. "You saw her eyes, didn't you? Those are not the eyes of a monster. They are the eyes of a woman bound by a curse far greater than the simple will to rule."

Darian's jaw clenched as he remembered the way Esmeray had looked at him, the flicker of vulnerability that had crossed her face. Her eyes had been fierce, yes, but there had been pain there too, something ancient and raw. Despite himself, he felt a strange urge to understand her, to peel back the layers of ice and see what lay beneath.

"What are you saying?" Darian asked, his voice barely above a whisper.

Thorian's gaze softened slightly, and he sighed. "I am saying that Esmeray is not the tyrant you believe her to be. She is a queen forced to make difficult choices, a woman bound by a curse that has taken far more from her than you could ever imagine." He paused, his expression unreadable. "If you truly wish to end her reign, then proceed. But know that doing so will not bring the peace you seek."

Darian stared at Thorian, his mind a whirlwind of conflicting emotions. He wanted to dismiss the advisor's words, to focus solely on his mission, but the memory of Esmeray's gaze lingered, haunting him.

As if sensing his turmoil, Thorian inclined his head slightly. "Perhaps you should return to the courtyard at dawn, when she appears as dragon. See if your convictions are as unshakable then."

Darian frowned, not quite understanding. "Why?"

Thorian's gaze was solemn. "Because sometimes, to understand a person, you must witness them in the light of their solitude."

Without waiting for a reply, Thorian turned and vanished into the shadows, leaving Darian alone in the icy courtyard. Darian's hand fell to his side, the cold weight of doubt settling over him like the snow that dusted the ground.

He turned back to the palace, his eyes tracing the intricate patterns of ice that formed its walls, the soft gleam of moonlight casting Esmeray's domain in an ethereal glow. He couldn't deny that there was a strange beauty here, a beauty that reflected its queen. Cold, remote, but captivating.

Unwilling to leave the palace, he made his way to a corner of the courtyard, where he could watch the moonlight shimmer on the ice. And as he settled into his temporary perch, he found himself lost in thoughts of Esmeray—the way she had appeared, fierce and proud, a queen who bore the weight of her power like a mantle of ice.

The memory of her gaze lingered, and though he tried to brush it aside, the sensation that had filled him when he'd looked into her eyes remained, a quiet warmth that contradicted the freezing night air.

Hours passed, and as dawn approached, Darian grew restless. He heard a soft rustling sound behind him and turned to see Esmeray standing at the entrance of the courtyard, her gaze fixed on him, her expression unreadable. She wore the same silver gown, its fabric rippling softly as the cold wind brushed through it.

"Couldn't stay away, could you?" she said, a trace of amusement in her voice as she approached.

Darian stood, his gaze locked on her. "I was... waiting," he replied, a hint of uncertainty in his voice.

She tilted her head, a ghost of a smile flickering across her lips. "Waiting for what, dragon slayer? To watch me turn back into the dragon you came to kill?"

Darian felt his heart skip a beat at her words, the reminder of his mission hanging heavily in the air. But as he looked at her, standing there with a mixture of defiance and vulnerability, the memory of his purpose seemed to waver.

"I thought... I thought I knew what I came here to do," he said, his voice barely above a whisper. "But I don't think I understand you at all, Esmeray."

A brief, wistful look crossed her face, her eyes softening. "Perhaps that is because you came here to kill a monster, and yet you found a queen." Her gaze held his, and for a heartbeat, the distance between them felt like a thread pulled taut, connecting them.

Without thinking, he reached for her hand, his fingers brushing against hers. Her skin was cold to the touch, but she didn't pull away. For a moment, they stood in silence, the palace around them disappearing as their gazes held, something unspoken passing between them.

Esmeray's voice was soft, almost wistful. "You should go, Darian. You came here to end my reign, and yet... here you stand, unsure of who I am."

"Maybe I don't want to kill you," Darian whispered, his fingers tightening around hers. "Maybe I want to understand you, Esmeray."

She hesitated, her eyes searching his. The cold distance between them seemed to melt away, replaced by a warmth that filled the space like a fragile spark. For the first time, her icy mask slipped, and he saw her—truly saw her—as a woman burdened by a curse she hadn't chosen, a queen who had sacrificed everything for her kingdom.

Esmeray's gaze dropped, and her lips curved into a faint, bittersweet smile. "Then perhaps... you should stay."

The words hung between them, a quiet invitation that felt as fragile as it was powerful. Darian's heart raced, a strange warmth filling him as he looked at her, this queen who was both dragon and woman, both powerful and vulnerable.

He knew, in that moment, that his mission had changed.

A Queen's Challenge

Dawn's first light cast a soft, ethereal glow over the Ice Queen's palace, transforming the frozen spires and walls into shimmering pillars of light and shadow. Darian stood in the courtyard, his breath fogging in the cold air, his thoughts racing after the previous night's encounter. He had come here with a singular mission—to end Esmeray's reign, to bring peace to the lands plagued by her dragons. But after standing face-to-face with her, feeling the subtle tremor of vulnerability behind her icy gaze, he felt as if he were straddling two worlds: the familiar hatred of a dragon slayer and an unfamiliar, growing fascination with the queen.

Just as the confusion was settling into his bones, a figure appeared at the far end of the courtyard. Darian's heart quickened as Esmeray stepped forward, her silver gown trailing behind her, reflecting the morning light like rippling water. She carried herself with a cold elegance, her expression unreadable as her gaze settled on him, her piercing blue eyes a stark contrast to the gentle dawn.

"Still here, I see," she said, her voice smooth, as though she were commenting on the weather. "I would have thought a dragon slayer would know better than to linger in enemy territory."

Darian tensed, his hand instinctively going to the hilt of his sword. He had expected a confrontation, a battle in her dragon form, but she looked at him not with the disdain he had anticipated, but with something closer to curiosity.

"I'm here to end your reign," he replied, though his voice lacked its previous conviction. "But you know that already."

Esmeray's lips curved into a slight, mocking smile. "Ah, yes. The hero, come to save the lands from the cruel Ice Queen." She took a step closer, her gaze fixed on him. "Tell me, Darian, have you ever stopped to wonder why I rule as I do?"

Darian's hand tightened on his sword. "Does it matter? You've terrorized the southern lands, expanded your borders with fear and fire. That's reason enough."

"Fear and fire," she echoed softly, her eyes narrowing as she studied him. "And yet you stand here, sword in hand, still unable to strike."

Darian opened his mouth to respond, but his words caught in his throat. She was right; he had hesitated. He had seen her transform from dragon to human and had felt something shift inside him, a strange sense of connection that made him question everything he thought he knew about her.

Esmeray let out a low, humorless laugh, taking another step closer, close enough that he could see the fine lines of frost that edged her lashes. "So tell me, dragon slayer," she continued, her voice dropping to a near-whisper. "What stops you? Is it fear, or... something else?"

Darian's heart pounded, his mind a storm of conflicting emotions. He had faced countless dragons, creatures of raw fury and power, but none had ever looked at him with such intensity. Her gaze held a challenge, daring him to look past her icy exterior and see the truth buried beneath. He tightened his grip on his sword, yet he made no move to draw it, caught between duty and an inexplicable draw toward her.

"I came here to kill a monster," he said, his voice rough, "but you're not what I expected."

Esmeray's expression softened just a fraction, though her gaze remained cold and calculating. "Then let me make it simple for you," she murmured, her voice laced with challenge. "I am offering you a choice. Prove yourself—strike me down, here and now. Or walk away. But if you choose to stay, know this: you will never be the same."

Darian's pulse quickened at her words. She was daring him, inviting him to face the truth of his own conflicted heart. Every instinct told him to fight, to strike before she turned back into the dragon. But the thought of cutting her down felt... wrong. He took a breath, his gaze locked with hers, and he lowered his hand from his sword, letting it fall to his side.

Esmeray's expression shifted, a flicker of surprise crossing her features. For a moment, they stood in silence, each waiting for the other to speak, as if the air between them held unspoken words and unacknowledged truths. The challenge in her eyes softened, and her lips parted slightly, as though she were about to say something. But then, just as quickly, she closed herself off, her expression hardening.

"You hesitate," she said, though there was no mockery in her tone this time. "Is it because you believe there's more to me than the legends?"

Darian hesitated, caught off guard by the quiet vulnerability in her voice. "I… I don't know what I believe anymore," he admitted, his voice barely above a whisper. "But I do know that what I see in front of me isn't a monster."

She stepped closer, her gaze softer now, her voice barely a whisper. "Then why are you here?"

The question hung in the air, and in that moment, he felt as if he were standing on the edge of a cliff, teetering between duty and a feeling he couldn't quite name. He searched her face, the hint of pain behind her cold demeanor, the unspoken sorrow that seemed to linger in her gaze. Something within him ached to reach out, to touch her, to understand the woman beneath the armor of ice.

"Maybe I came here to understand you," he murmured, his voice barely audible.

Esmeray's breath caught, and for a heartbeat, she looked at him with a vulnerability that took his breath away. Her gaze flickered to his hand, the one that had been resting on his sword, and she reached out, her fingers brushing against his, the contact cold yet electric. The warmth of his skin seemed to radiate through her, melting something deep within her that she had thought long dead.

"Then you are more a fool than I thought," she whispered, though her voice held no malice. Her fingers lingered against his, her touch hesitant, as though she were afraid to let herself feel the warmth of his skin.

Darian's heart pounded, his every instinct telling him to pull back, to remember his mission. But he couldn't. His fingers curled around hers, holding her hand gently as if afraid she might disappear. "If I am a fool," he whispered, "then you are the one who made me so."

A faint blush colored her cheeks, and she looked down, a hint of uncertainty breaking through her usual composure. Her hand trembled slightly in his grasp, but she didn't pull away. Instead, she looked back up at him, her gaze searching his, as though trying to understand the man who had come here to kill her yet now held her hand as if she were something precious.

"You are brave, Darian," she murmured, her voice barely above a whisper. "Brave, but foolish. This bond you feel… it will lead you nowhere but ruin."

Darian shook his head, his grip tightening on her hand. "Then let it ruin me," he replied, his voice filled with a quiet intensity. "Because I don't think I could leave now, even if I wanted to."

Esmeray's lips parted, her eyes widening at his words. She took a step closer, her hand still clasped in his, and he could feel her breath against his skin, a faint chill that sent a shiver through him. Her gaze softened, her walls crumbling just a bit more, and in that moment, he saw her for who she truly was—a woman bound by a curse, a queen forced to rule with an iron fist, a soul burdened by centuries of solitude.

"You don't understand what you're asking for," she whispered, her voice trembling. "This bond between us… it can only end in heartbreak."

"Then let it break me," he murmured, his thumb brushing over her fingers. "Because whatever this is, whatever lies between us… I'd rather face it than live the rest of my life wondering what might have been."

Esmeray closed her eyes, her face softening, and for a moment, Darian thought she might finally let down her guard. But then she opened her eyes, her expression hardening once more, though her hand remained in his.

"Then prove yourself, dragon slayer," she said, her voice a mixture of challenge and desperation. "If you truly believe there is more to me than the legends, then show me. Show me that you are willing to see beyond the curse, beyond the fear."

Darian's heart pounded, his every instinct screaming at him to retreat, to end this before it was too late. But he couldn't pull away. Instead, he stepped closer, his gaze locked with hers, the distance between them shrinking until there was nothing left but the quiet hum of tension that filled the air.

Slowly, he lifted her hand, bringing it to his lips. His breath was warm against her skin, and he felt her shiver, a tremor that spoke of vulnerability, of walls beginning to crack. "I will prove it," he whispered against her hand, his voice steady. "I will prove that you are more than just a curse."

Esmeray's breath hitched, her gaze softening as she looked at him, her hand still held in his. For a heartbeat, he saw the woman behind the queen, the woman who had been hidden away behind layers of ice and duty. Her lips parted as if to speak, but instead, she simply looked at him, a mixture of fear and longing in her eyes.

"Then perhaps, dragon slayer," she murmured, her voice trembling, "you are not so foolish after all."

Their gazes lingered, and for the first time, Darian felt the weight of his purpose dissolve into something softer, something warmer. Esmeray's icy blue eyes held his, and he saw the traces of vulnerability there, the shadows of an unspoken sorrow that seemed to reach out to him. His hand still held hers, their fingers entwined in a way that felt so natural, so right, as if this simple contact could bridge the vast chasm between them.

"Esmeray…" he whispered, his voice hushed, as if afraid to break the fragile moment between them. He could feel her pulse fluttering beneath his fingertips, her steady resolve flickering as her gaze softened. It was as if a mask had fallen away, leaving only the woman beneath—the woman he found himself captivated by, despite every warning, every reason to hold back.

She drew in a shaky breath, her lips parting as if to speak, but no words came. Instead, her gaze fell to where their hands were clasped, her fingers slowly curling to fit against his. She looked up at him, her expression wavering between fear and hope, her carefully constructed walls visibly beginning to crack.

"I shouldn't let this happen," she murmured, her voice barely above a whisper. Her gaze flickered down, her fingers pressing gently against his palm.

"Darian, you don't know what you're asking for... what this could mean."

Darian stepped closer, closing the already small distance between them, his other hand lifting to gently touch her cheek. Her skin was cool beneath his fingers, like the first chill of winter, but it softened as he stroked her cheek, drawing her closer. His thumb brushed against her cheekbone, and he felt a faint tremor run through her, a response she didn't seem able to control.

"I know exactly what I'm asking," he murmured, his voice a steady whisper. "I'm asking for a chance... a chance to understand the woman behind the queen."

A flicker of doubt flashed in her eyes, but her hand remained in his, her fingers tightening slightly as if she were afraid to let go. "I am bound to this land, Darian," she whispered, her voice trembling. "I am as much a part of this ice and snow as the mountains themselves. This... whatever it is between us... it can only end in pain."

His thumb continued to trace gentle circles against her cheek. "Then let it be pain. I'd rather feel that, if it means I got to know you... to truly know you."

Her breath caught, and she looked up at him, her eyes searching his face for any trace of doubt, any hint that he might falter. But all she found was a quiet determination, a gentleness she had never expected to see in the eyes of a dragon slayer. Slowly, as if against her own resolve, she leaned into his touch, her face tilting toward his, her eyes fluttering closed as her guard finally crumbled.

Darian's hand slid around to the back of her neck, his fingers threading through the soft tendrils of her hair, and he felt her shiver beneath his touch. Her breathing grew uneven, her lips parting ever so slightly as he closed the remaining distance between them. He leaned down, his face mere inches from hers, and he could feel her breath, cold yet intoxicating, as it mingled with his own.

"Esmeray," he whispered again, her name falling from his lips like a quiet promise. She opened her eyes, and for a heartbeat, they simply looked at each other, neither willing to break the delicate tension that held them together.

But then, almost instinctively, he tilted his head, closing the distance between them as his lips brushed softly against hers. The touch was light, tentative, as if they were testing the waters, exploring a connection neither had anticipated. Esmeray's lips were cool, a sensation that sent a shiver down his spine, but as she leaned into him, her mouth softened, her kiss warming as she returned it.

Their kiss deepened, slow and tender, each movement careful, as if they were afraid to break the spell. Darian felt a fierce protectiveness rise within him, a need to shield her from whatever burdens weighed on her shoulders. His arms wrapped around her, pulling her closer, and she melted into his embrace, her fingers curling into the fabric of his cloak as though anchoring herself to him.

Esmeray's lips moved against his with a desperation she hadn't allowed herself to feel in centuries, as though she were pouring all her sorrow, her longing, and her loneliness into this single, stolen moment. For the first time in so long, she felt something other than the cold solitude of her curse; she felt warmth, radiating from him, enveloping her like a fire that refused to be extinguished.

When they finally broke apart, their foreheads rested together, their breaths mingling in the chilled air. She looked up at him, her eyes wide and filled with a vulnerability that made his heart ache. She lifted a hand to his face, her fingers tracing the rough line of his jaw, and her touch was gentle, reverent, as if she couldn't quite believe he was real.

"Why, Darian?" she whispered, her voice wavering. "Why are you here, willing to give up everything… for someone like me?"

He held her gaze, his thumb brushing against her cheek as he searched for the words to express what he was feeling. "Because I see you, Esmeray. Not the queen, not the dragon. I see you—the woman trapped beneath it all. And… I want to free you from that."

Her eyes filled with unshed tears, and she looked away, her voice barely a whisper. "I don't deserve to be saved."

He lifted her chin, gently guiding her gaze back to his. "You do, Esmeray," he said, his voice firm yet tender. "Whatever the past may hold, whatever mistakes or regrets haunt you, you deserve a chance to live freely. To feel, to be loved."

A tear slipped down her cheek, and she let out a shaky breath, her fingers tightening around his as though she were afraid to let go. "I haven't allowed myself to feel… anything… in so long," she admitted, her voice cracking. "The curse has forced me to live as a dragon, to rule with coldness, to forsake love. And yet here you are, breaking through every wall I've built."

Darian leaned closer, his forehead resting gently against hers. "Then let those walls fall," he whispered, his voice a soft plea. "Let me show you that there's more than just ice and solitude. You don't have to carry this burden alone."

Esmeray's fingers brushed his cheek, her touch soft, as though she were memorizing the feel of his skin beneath her fingertips. Her lips quivered, and for a moment, she looked at him as though he were her only tether to reality. She pulled him closer, their lips meeting again, and this time, the kiss was deeper, more passionate, as if she were surrendering herself to the warmth he offered.

The world around them faded, the cold of the morning forgotten as they lost themselves in each other. Darian's hand slipped to her waist, pulling her against him as she responded to his kiss with an intensity that took his breath away. Her hands tangled in his hair, pulling him closer, as if she couldn't bear to let him go.

When they finally broke apart, both were breathless, their hearts racing as they looked at each other, the silence between them filled with a thousand unspoken promises. Darian's thumb brushed the last of her tears away, and he gave her a small, reassuring smile.

"Stay," she whispered, the word filled with a quiet, aching vulnerability that tugged at his heart. "Please, stay."

He held her tightly, his arms wrapped around her as he nodded, his own voice rough with emotion. "I'm not going anywhere, Esmeray. Not anymore."

For the first time, the Ice Queen let herself lean into him fully, her body relaxing against his as though finally allowing herself to trust, to let down the defenses she'd kept for centuries. And in that quiet embrace, they found a fragile, precious peace, a warmth that banished the cold for a single, perfect moment.

The Dragon's Curse

The palace was bathed in the silver glow of the moon, casting intricate patterns on the ice walls that gleamed like crystal. In the quiet stillness, Esmeray sat alone in her chambers, gazing out over the frozen expanse of her kingdom. The heavy silence of the night had always been her only true companion, a reminder of the centuries she had spent in isolation, bound by the curse that forced her to shift between forms each day and night.

As she leaned against the chilled window frame, Esmeray's thoughts drifted to the day's events—the unexpected connection with Darian, his touch, the warmth that had momentarily melted through her carefully guarded defenses. She lifted a trembling hand to her cheek, as if she could still feel the gentle brush of his fingers, the way he had looked at her as though he could see through her icy exterior to the woman hidden beneath.

Her eyes drifted closed, her mind casting back to the night that had changed her life forever, the night she had been bound to this curse.

Centuries ago, she had been young, idealistic, and full of love. Her heart had belonged to someone she had believed in, someone who had promised her the world. But he had betrayed her, leaving her to shoulder the burdens of a kingdom torn by war. His betrayal had cut deep, shattering her heart and leaving scars that had yet to heal. And in her moment of despair and grief, a powerful sorceress had offered her a choice: to wield her pain as power, to cast aside her humanity and bind herself to the elements of ice and snow, to become something untouchable.

Esmeray had taken the offer, sealing her heart in a fortress of ice, believing that by forsaking love, she could rule without weakness, without the vulnerability that had once brought her to her knees. The curse had made her powerful, had turned her into the Ice Queen feared by all. Yet every sunrise forced her into the form of a dragon, a creature of strength and fury, an outward manifestation of the walls she had built around her heart.

But now, for the first time in centuries, she was beginning to doubt the worth of her power. The look in Darian's eyes, the way he had held her, as though she were more than a queen bound by magic—it had stirred something in her, something she had long since buried.

A quiet knock on the door interrupted her thoughts, and she turned, her heart unexpectedly quickening at the thought that it might be him. She hesitated, then lifted her chin and called out, "Enter."

The door creaked open, and Darian stepped into the room, his expression soft as he took in her figure silhouetted against the moonlight. She turned away, her hands clasping together tightly, trying to mask the flutter of emotions his presence ignited.

"Couldn't sleep?" he asked, his voice low, as he moved closer, stopping a respectful distance away.

Esmeray forced herself to adopt her usual cool demeanor, though the effort felt forced. "Sleep does not come easily to those who bear the weight of a kingdom," she replied, her voice steady. She glanced at him over her shoulder, noting the way his gaze lingered on her, his eyes filled with a mixture of curiosity and… something else, something softer.

Darian took a step closer, his gaze unwavering. "I would think that even a queen could use rest now and then," he said quietly, his voice laced with genuine concern.

Esmeray's lips quirked into a faint, bitter smile. "You forget that I am no ordinary queen," she murmured. "My nights are spent in a form bound to this kingdom, just as my days are spent under the weight of my curse."

Darian's brow furrowed as he absorbed her words, his gaze darkening with something close to sympathy. "This curse… it forces you to become a dragon each day?"

She nodded, her expression tightening as memories surfaced, memories she had tried so hard to bury. "Yes. Each dawn, I become the creature that has come to define me—the Ice Queen, feared and powerful. And with each sunset, I am reminded of the woman I once was, the woman who was foolish enough to believe in love."

Darian's expression softened, and he moved a step closer, his voice gentle. "Esmeray… what happened to you? Why this curse?"

She turned away, her shoulders tense, her fingers tightening against the windowsill. "It was a choice I made," she replied quietly, her voice carrying the weight of centuries of pain. "I was once in love, Darian. I trusted him, believed in him with all my heart. And he betrayed me, abandoned me when I needed him most."

Darian's fists clenched at his sides, his jaw tightening. "I'm sorry, Esmeray. No one deserves that."

A bitter laugh escaped her, and she shook her head. "Perhaps not. But it taught me a valuable lesson—that love is nothing more than a weakness, a weapon that can be wielded against you. So I took my pain and turned it into power. The curse gave me strength, the kind that could never be shaken by love or betrayal."

Darian reached out, his hand gently resting on her shoulder. "Esmeray… that isn't strength. That's a prison."

She flinched at his words, her icy composure faltering. His touch, warm and steady, seemed to seep through the cracks in her walls, thawing the frozen edges of her heart. She felt her breath catch as his fingers traced the line of her shoulder, his warmth bleeding through the cold that had defined her for so long.

"I have ruled for centuries, Darian," she whispered, her voice tinged with a quiet desperation. "I've kept my kingdom safe, protected my people. I thought that was enough… that it would be enough. But now… now I don't know."

He turned her gently to face him, his hands resting on her shoulders, grounding her. "Esmeray, you don't have to face this alone. I see the strength in you, the weight you bear, but I also see the woman beneath it all—the woman who still feels, who still hopes, even if she tries to hide it."

She looked up at him, her heart pounding as his words unraveled her defenses. The vulnerability in his gaze, the quiet acceptance of everything she was, left her feeling both exposed and cherished in a way she hadn't allowed herself to feel in centuries.

"And what do you see, Darian?" she whispered, her voice trembling. "When you look at me, what do you see?"

He brushed a strand of hair from her face, his touch sending a shiver down her spine. "I see a woman who has been forced to be strong for too long. A queen who bears the weight of a kingdom but is also bound by her own pain. And I see someone who deserves a chance to be free."

A tear slipped down her cheek, and she looked away, ashamed of the raw emotion that she couldn't hide. But he lifted her chin, his gaze unwavering as he looked at her, his own eyes reflecting a depth of feeling that took her breath away.

"You don't have to be cold forever, Esmeray," he murmured. "Let me be the warmth you need."

His words were a balm to her wounded heart, the promise of something she had long believed lost. She reached up, her hand resting on his cheek, her thumb brushing over his rough stubble as she allowed herself to feel the warmth of his skin.

"I want to believe you, Darian," she whispered, her voice a soft confession. "I want to believe that there can be more for me than this curse."

He leaned closer, his forehead resting gently against hers, their breaths mingling in the silence of the room. "Then believe, Esmeray. Let yourself trust again. I will be here, no matter how hard it may seem."

They stood there, wrapped in a quiet intimacy that defied the centuries of loneliness she had endured. And as he closed the remaining distance between them, his lips brushing softly against hers, she felt something shift within her—a tiny spark, a flicker of hope that melted the ice around her heart.

The kiss was slow and tender, filled with a promise she hadn't dared to believe in. His lips were warm, a gentle contrast to the chill that had always surrounded her, and she leaned into him, allowing herself to feel, to let down her guard. His hands slid around her waist, pulling her close, and she surrendered, letting herself be vulnerable, if only for this moment.

When they finally broke apart, he rested his forehead against hers, his breath steady and reassuring. She looked up at him, her gaze filled with wonder, a quiet awe at the tenderness he offered her without condition.

"Darian," she whispered, her voice barely audible. "I don't know how to do this… to open myself to someone."

He gave her a soft smile, his thumb tracing gentle circles on her back. "Then let me show you, one step at a time."

A tear slipped down her cheek, and for the first time, she didn't feel the need to hide it. She let herself lean into him, her head resting against his chest, feeling the warmth of his embrace, the steady beat of his heart beneath her ear. And in that quiet, fragile moment, she allowed herself to hope that maybe, just maybe, she could be more than the Ice Queen.

Maybe, with Darian by her side, she could find her way back to the woman she had once been—the woman who had loved and trusted and believed in something greater than power. And as they stood there, entwined in each other's arms, Esmeray felt the walls around her heart begin to crumble, piece by frozen piece.

A Dance of Fire and Ice

The castle was silent, draped in shadows and moonlight as the night deepened. Its ice-covered walls glistened with a cold beauty that seemed almost alive, each room a chamber of secrets held by the Ice Queen herself. Darian, restless after yet another sleepless night, roamed the halls, his thoughts a tangled web of duty, curiosity, and something far more dangerous: attraction.

He turned a corner, only to find a figure standing by one of the tall arched windows, her silhouette framed in silver light. It was Esmeray, lost in thought as she stared out over her kingdom, her posture both regal and solitary.

He hesitated, not wanting to disturb her, but her gaze snapped to him, her expression unreadable.

"Awake so late, dragon slayer?" she asked, her voice as smooth and cool as the ice surrounding them. She turned fully to face him, her gown of silvery fabric flowing around her like a whisper of moonlight.

"I could ask the same of you," Darian replied, stepping closer. "Though I suspect you're used to the night. It suits you."

A faint smirk tugged at her lips. "It suits my curse, not me. My days are spent as a dragon; my nights, as this." She motioned to herself, her gaze steady, but there was a flicker of vulnerability that intrigued him even more.

"And which form is the true one?" he asked, moving closer, his voice low. "The dragon, or the queen?"

Esmeray's gaze hardened, though he caught a trace of amusement in her eyes. "Do you always ask such personal questions, or is it only with me?"

"Maybe it's only with you," he said, undeterred. "After all, you're not exactly a typical ruler."

"Neither are you a typical dragon slayer," she countered, her voice a mixture of challenge and curiosity. "You seem to have a dangerous fascination with a woman you came to kill."

Darian chuckled, crossing his arms. "Maybe I'm just testing my strength against yours, seeing how close I can get to the flames before they consume me."

Esmeray took a step forward, her eyes gleaming as if accepting his challenge. "Then you should be careful, dragon slayer. My fire can burn."

Their eyes held, the space between them charged with tension, when a quiet cough from the shadows broke the silence. Both turned to see a slender figure watching them, a look of dry amusement on his face. Thorian, Esmeray's trusted advisor, leaned casually against the wall, his arms crossed.

"I see the castle has become a playground for dangerous flirtation," Thorian remarked, his voice dripping with a sarcasm that seemed to amuse Esmeray. "Should I leave you two alone, or perhaps I should remind you, Your Majesty, that entertaining dragon slayers might not be the best use of your time?"

Esmeray shot him a sharp look, though her lips quirked into a faint smile. "Thorian, I thought you were better at minding your own business."

Thorian shrugged, pushing off the wall and strolling toward them with the easy grace of someone who'd been in her life for years. "You know how I am, my queen. If I minded my own business, this castle would have fallen apart long ago." His gaze slid to Darian, a brow raised. "And who knows what might happen with a dragon slayer wandering the halls at night."

Darian chuckled, amused by Thorian's boldness. "You're not worried about your queen, are you?"

Thorian studied him, his expression unreadable. "I don't worry about my queen. I trust her," he said pointedly, his gaze lingering on Darian. "But I am protective of her. I've seen enough betrayal to recognize the signs, and I would hate for history to repeat itself."

Esmeray's gaze softened, a rare look of affection in her eyes as she glanced at Thorian. "We all know history repeats itself one way or another," she said quietly, a trace of sorrow in her tone. "But Thorian is right to be wary." She turned to Darian, her gaze once again guarded. "People rarely come into my life with pure intentions, dragon slayer."

Darian felt a pang at her words, but he held her gaze, determined. "I won't pretend that I didn't come here with a mission, Esmeray. But things have changed."

"Have they?" she asked, her voice quiet but tinged with curiosity. "Or are you simply drawn to the idea of taming the Ice Queen?"

Darian moved closer, his voice a murmur. "Maybe I am. Maybe I think there's something behind all this ice worth melting."

Esmeray's breath caught, her composure slipping just slightly, but Thorian cleared his throat, breaking the moment.

"Well," Thorian said, his tone dry. "If you two are going to carry on like this, you might as well do so in a way that befits royalty." He gestured toward the open hall beyond, where a large, elegant chamber waited. Its floor was smooth as glass, reflecting the moonlight streaming in through the arched windows.

"A dance, then?" Esmeray asked, arching a brow as she glanced between Darian and Thorian. Her gaze settled on Darian, a glint of amusement sparking in her eyes. "Do you know how to dance, dragon slayer?"

Darian extended his hand, his eyes glinting with challenge. "Care to find out?"

Esmeray placed her hand in his, allowing him to pull her into the open hall. Thorian stood by, leaning against the wall with an amused smile as he watched them take their positions. Darian's hand settled on her waist, his touch warm against her cool skin. He could feel the tension in her posture, the way she held herself with a rigid control that betrayed her reluctance.

"Relax," he murmured, his voice soft but commanding. "I won't bite."

She shot him a sardonic smile. "I'm more concerned about myself, dragon slayer. I might burn you."

Darian laughed, his hand guiding her into the first steps of a slow, deliberate dance. "Then I'll take the risk."

They began to move, each step a subtle battle of wills, a clash of fire and ice. Esmeray moved with a grace that was both commanding and elegant, her every movement calculated, her gaze unwavering.

But Darian matched her, refusing to yield, his hand guiding her with a confidence that seemed to both challenge and intrigue her.

Their eyes met, and the tension between them crackled, the air thick with unspoken words, lingering touches, and the silent promise of something deeper.

"You don't make this easy," she murmured, her gaze steady.

"Did you expect me to?" he replied, his voice a soft rumble as he spun her, drawing her close again. "Or is that what you want?"

A faint blush colored her cheeks, and she looked away, a flicker of uncertainty breaking through her composed facade. "I don't know what I want," she admitted quietly, her voice barely audible. "Not anymore."

Darian's hand tightened on her waist, his gaze softening as he looked at her. "Then maybe it's time to stop fighting so hard. Let yourself feel, Esmeray. You don't have to be the Ice Queen with me."

Her breath hitched at his words, and for a moment, she looked up at him with an expression so vulnerable it took his breath away. But then she caught herself, her walls snapping back into place as she gave him a wry smile. "And what would you do if I were to let you in, Darian? You're a dragon slayer. I'm a dragon. The story doesn't exactly end in happily ever after."

Darian's gaze turned serious, his hand sliding to her lower back as he pulled her even closer. "Maybe we don't need a happily ever after. Maybe we just need now."

Their faces were inches apart, her cool breath brushing against his lips as he leaned closer, the tension between them unbearable. But before he could close the distance, Thorian cleared his throat, reminding them of his presence.

"I hate to interrupt this little… interlude," Thorian said, though his expression was both amused and resigned, "but I do believe, Your Majesty, you have other matters to attend to." He looked at Darian, a hint of warning in his eyes. "And you, dragon slayer, have an early start in the morning, I presume."

Darian exhaled, pulling back from Esmeray reluctantly, his gaze lingering on her. "Until next time, then," he murmured, his voice filled with a quiet promise.

Esmeray nodded, her gaze lingering on him with a mixture of longing and apprehension. "Next time," she replied, her voice barely above a whisper.

As Darian turned to leave, he felt a pang of regret, a sense that he was leaving something unfinished, something fragile and precious. But as he glanced back, he saw Esmeray watching him, her eyes filled with an emotion that mirrored his own.

Thorian's voice broke the silence, his tone quiet and somber. "Be careful, Darian," he murmured. "This path you're treading... it may lead to ruin."

Darian nodded, his gaze resolute. "I know. But for her... I'm willing to risk it."

With that, he walked away, leaving Esmeray and Thorian behind. And as he disappeared into the shadows, he knew that he was falling into something deeper, something that could change everything—for better or for worse.

The Hunter and the Hunted

The sun rose over the icy peaks of the northern mountains, casting its pale light over the frozen landscape below. Darian stood at the edge of a cliff, the biting wind tugging at his cloak as he watched Esmeray's dragon form stretch across the sky, her white scales glinting in the morning light. She was a sight to behold, her wings slicing through the frigid air with both power and grace. What once had seemed like a monstrous form now appeared to him as something wild and beautiful—a creature bound by her own strength and solitude.

For so long, he had viewed dragons as creatures to be feared, beasts to be slain. But watching Esmeray's dragon form as she soared above her kingdom, he found himself transfixed, unable to look away. The dragon, he realized, was no mindless beast but an extension of her—the same soul, burdened with centuries of memories and pain, locked in a form that was equal parts freedom and prison.

As he watched her glide through the morning light, his thoughts drifted to the night they'd shared, the quiet moments that had unraveled something deep within him. She was a queen with a heart guarded by steel, a woman burdened by duty and heartbreak. But beyond her defenses, he'd glimpsed the person she kept hidden. And now, he couldn't shake the feeling that there was something worth saving, something that called to him more than his duty ever could.

"Quite the sight, isn't she?"

Darian turned to find Thorian standing beside him, his gaze fixed on the dragon with an expression of quiet reverence. Darian hesitated, then nodded, unable to mask his admiration.

"She is," he admitted softly. "There's a... sadness to it. Like she's searching for something she's lost."

Thorian's mouth curved into a faint, bittersweet smile. "That's the curse, isn't it?" he murmured. "To soar above your own kingdom, but to never truly be free. She flies each morning not out of joy, but out of duty. A reminder of the power she wields, of the pain she's endured."

Darian swallowed, his gaze drifting back to Esmeray as she dipped low over the mountainside, her massive wings casting shadows over the ice. "She spoke of betrayal," he said, his voice quiet. "Something that drove her to take on this curse."

Thorian's expression hardened slightly, his gaze flickering with something unspoken. "Yes. A betrayal that left her with nothing but ashes and scars." He turned to Darian, his eyes sharp. "Esmeray has been hurt by those she trusted. She has learned to wield her pain as a shield. But don't mistake her strength for indifference. She feels,

Darian. She feels more deeply than you could imagine."

Darian's jaw clenched, the weight of Thorian's words settling over him. "Then why does she push everyone away?" he asked, frustration creeping into his tone. "Why keep herself locked away in ice and silence?"

Thorian sighed, his gaze distant. "Because to open herself would mean risking that pain again. It would mean making herself vulnerable, and vulnerability has brought her nothing but heartache. She chose this curse because it allowed her to protect herself and her kingdom… at a cost."

Darian's hands tightened into fists as he watched Esmeray circle back, her dragon form gliding effortlessly through the air. "There has to be a way to free her," he murmured, more to himself than to Thorian.

Thorian regarded him with a solemn expression. "You're playing with fire, dragon slayer. Esmeray is not the kind of woman who lets go of her defenses easily. She has become so much a part of this curse that she may not know how to break free, even if she wanted to."

Darian nodded, though a sense of determination burned within him. "Maybe," he said quietly. "But she deserves the chance to try."

They stood in silence, watching as Esmeray dove through the air, her form a flash of silver against the clear blue sky. But then, suddenly, she banked sharply, her massive wings tilting as she noticed them on the cliff edge below. Her gaze found Darian's, and even from this distance, he could feel the weight of her stare, a mixture of wariness and something else... something raw and unspoken.

With a powerful beat of her wings, she descended, her form growing larger as she approached. Darian's heart raced as she landed gracefully on the cliffside, the ground shuddering slightly beneath the weight of her powerful body. She folded her wings, her gaze piercing as she regarded him in silence.

"Darian," she said, her voice low, a rumbling growl that echoed through the mountain air. Even in her dragon form, her words carried a chilling authority, a reminder of the power that pulsed within her.

He took a step closer, his hand instinctively resting on the hilt of his sword, though he had no intention of drawing it. "Esmeray," he replied, his voice steady. "I wanted to... I wanted to see you like this. To see the part of you that bears this curse."

Her dragon eyes narrowed, her gaze unyielding. "Why?" she demanded, her tone sharp. "To remind yourself of your mission? To remind yourself that I am the enemy?"

Darian shook his head, his eyes softening as he looked at her. "No. I came to understand."

A low growl escaped her, a sound that held more pain than fury. "You think you can understand, dragon slayer? You, who came here to kill me? You know nothing of what it means to be bound to this form, to live as a creature feared and despised."

He took another step forward, undeterred by her towering form. "Then help me understand, Esmeray. Show me what it is you fear."

Her gaze softened slightly, though her voice remained guarded. "Why do you want to know, Darian? Why do you care?"

He hesitated, struggling to find the words that would convey the turmoil in his heart. "Because," he said slowly, his voice filled with a quiet determination, "I've come to see more than just a queen bound by a curse. I've seen the woman beneath, the one who fights so hard to keep herself hidden. And I can't ignore that. Not anymore."

She studied him in silence, her gaze intense, as if weighing the sincerity of his words. Slowly, she lowered her massive head, her eyes level with his, her voice softer, more vulnerable.

"You're a fool, dragon slayer," she murmured, her tone laced with both sadness and admiration. "You risk everything to draw close to me, and for what? I am cursed, bound to this form. I am not the queen you think you see. I am only… this."

Darian lifted a hand, hesitating as he reached toward her, his fingers trembling slightly. Her gaze flickered with both fear and curiosity, but she held still, allowing him to touch her. His fingers brushed against her scales, and he felt a strange warmth radiating from her, a warmth that defied the icy facade she wore.

"You are not just this," he whispered. "You are so much more."

Her breath hitched, and he felt a shudder run through her as she closed her eyes, allowing herself a rare moment of vulnerability. "Darian… if you knew the truth of this curse, if you saw the burden I carry, you would walk away. You would see that I am not worth the risk."

"Let me be the judge of that," he replied, his voice steady, his fingers trailing gently over her scales. "I've fought dragons, faced down impossible odds, but none of that prepared me for meeting you, Esmeray. You… you've changed everything I thought I knew."

Her eyes opened, and for a heartbeat, he saw the woman beneath the dragon, the queen who had sacrificed everything for her kingdom. "You are a strange man, Darian," she murmured. "A dragon slayer who doesn't want to kill."

He smiled, his hand lingering against her scales. "Maybe I came here to slay the wrong thing. Maybe I came here to destroy the walls you've built around your heart."

A faint laugh escaped her, a sound that was both bitter and wistful. "I don't know if that's possible, Darian. My heart… it's frozen, locked away where no one can reach it. Even I don't know if it can be thawed."

"Then let me try," he whispered, his gaze filled with a quiet, unyielding resolve. "Let me be the warmth you need."

She looked at him, her dragon form towering over him, yet in that moment, she seemed almost fragile, as though his words had struck a chord she hadn't expected. Slowly, she inclined her head, her gaze never leaving his.

"Perhaps," she said softly, her voice laced with uncertainty. "But be warned, Darian. If you venture too close to the fire, you may get burned."

Darian's lips curved into a small smile, his hand slipping from her scales. "Then let me burn, Esmeray. Because I would rather face that fire than live a life without ever truly knowing you."

Their eyes held, the air between them filled with a fragile tension that spoke of promises unspoken, emotions yet to be explored. And as the morning light painted the mountains in shades of gold and silver, Darian knew that he was no longer just a hunter, and she was no longer merely the hunted.

They were something more, bound together in a dance of fire and ice, each step drawing them closer to a truth that neither could deny.

Cracks in the Ice

The evenings in Esmeray's castle held a quiet beauty, a peace that felt almost unnatural in a place as cold and imposing as this. Each night, as the sun dipped behind the mountains and Esmeray's transformation to her human form was complete, she would wander the halls, seeking solace in the dimly lit spaces of her icy kingdom. And, almost as if by unspoken agreement, Darian would find her, their paths crossing in a delicate dance of tension and curiosity.

Tonight, Darian found her in the library—a grand hall filled with towering shelves of ancient tomes, the air thick with the scent of parchment and memories. Esmeray stood by a window, her gaze distant as she watched the world outside darken. Moonlight bathed her in a silvery glow, illuminating the soft lines of her face, the shadowed depths of her eyes. She looked almost serene, but Darian could sense the turmoil that simmered beneath her composed exterior.

"Another night, another vigil," he said softly as he approached, careful not to startle her.

She turned, her expression softening just a fraction as she regarded him. "Are you always this persistent, dragon slayer?" she asked, her tone light but with an edge of genuine curiosity.

"Only when the cause is worth it," he replied with a smile, stepping closer. "I've faced dragons, scaled mountains, yet here I am, captivated by a woman who seems to be made of both fire and ice."

Esmeray's lips curved in a faint smile, her gaze drifting to the floor. "Captivated?" she echoed, a note of disbelief in her voice. "I would think a man like you would be more wary of something as dangerous as me."

"Maybe that's exactly why I'm here," he murmured, his voice steady. "Because I see the woman behind the queen, the heart you try so hard to keep hidden."

Her smile faded, her eyes darkening as she turned back to the window, her voice soft. "It's dangerous, Darian, to seek warmth in something that was forged in the cold. You don't know what you're asking for."

Darian stepped closer, his hand resting gently on the windowsill beside her. "Then show me. Let me see the truth beneath all this ice."

She hesitated, her fingers brushing over the frost-covered windowsill as if tracing old memories. "It was so long ago," she whispered, her voice filled with a quiet sorrow. "I was young… foolish. I believed in love, in trust. But that trust was broken, shattered into a thousand pieces. And I took the only path I thought I had left."

Darian's heart ached as he listened, his gaze softening. "What happened, Esmeray? Who betrayed you?"

She closed her eyes, her breath shaky as she let herself drift into the past. "His name was Alaric. He was... everything to me. A powerful sorcerer, a man with a smile that could melt the very ice beneath our feet. I thought he loved me, thought he wanted to build a future together. But he used me—used my heart, my power, to strengthen his own. And when he had what he needed... he left, leaving me to the curse he'd helped cast."

Darian reached out, his hand covering hers in a gentle gesture of comfort. "You didn't deserve that. No one does."

She glanced down at their hands, a mixture of surprise and reluctance flashing across her face before she pulled her hand away, folding her arms protectively around herself. "It taught me a lesson I won't soon forget," she said, her tone hardening. "Love is nothing but a weapon that can be wielded against you. It's a weakness that I cannot afford."

Darian frowned, his gaze intense. "Love isn't a weakness, Esmeray. It's a strength. And you're not defined by what he did to you. You're stronger than that."

She looked at him, her gaze guarded but softening under his gentle words. "Strong, perhaps. But strength doesn't undo the curse. It doesn't change what I've become."

Darian stepped closer, his voice steady and filled with conviction. "What you've become is more than just this curse. You're a queen, a protector, a woman with a heart that still feels—no matter how much you try to hide it."

Her gaze wavered, her defenses beginning to crack. "Darian… I'm not the woman you want me to be. I am bound to this life, to this kingdom, to this curse. I can't let myself hope for anything more."

He reached out, his fingers gently brushing a stray lock of hair from her face. "Maybe you don't have to bear this alone. Maybe you're not as bound as you think."

Esmeray's eyes softened, a flicker of something vulnerable and raw crossing her face. For a moment, it seemed as though she might let him in, might allow herself to be seen in all her brokenness. But then she drew back, her walls rising once more as she hugged her arms around herself.

"You're a fool, dragon slayer," she murmured, though there was no malice in her tone. "A fool who sees only what he wants to see."

"Then let me be a fool," he whispered, his gaze unwavering. "If it means I get to know you… the real you."

A flicker of conflict crossed her face, and for a heartbeat, she looked as though she might take a step toward him, let down her defenses completely. But instead, she turned back to the window, her voice barely above a whisper.

"Tell me, Darian," she said, her tone wistful. "Do you ever wish things were different? That you hadn't come here to kill me?"

He hesitated, his own heart aching with the answer he could hardly admit to himself. "Yes," he said quietly. "Every day."

Her gaze softened, a faint, sad smile curving her lips. "Then maybe we're both fools."

They stood in silence, the weight of unspoken words hanging heavy between them, until finally, she spoke, her voice a quiet plea. "Will you stay? Just for tonight?"

Darian's breath caught, his heart pounding as he nodded. "Of course."

They sat by the fire, the warmth casting a soft glow over the room, their barriers lowered if only for this moment. They spoke of simple things, of memories and dreams, of fleeting moments of happiness she hadn't allowed herself to remember in years. And with each word, each quiet confession, he felt the cracks in her icy armor widen, revealing glimpses of the woman she'd once been—and the woman she might still become.

After a long pause, she looked at him, her gaze filled with a mixture of fear and hope. "I don't know how to do this, Darian," she whispered. "To let someone in again."

He reached out, his hand covering hers in a gesture of reassurance. "Then let me show you. One step at a time."

Her lips trembled, her gaze fixed on their hands as she nodded, a tear slipping down her cheek. He brushed it away with a tenderness that seemed to surprise her, his thumb lingering against her skin as he held her gaze.

"Darian," she murmured, her voice filled with a vulnerability that tore at his heart. "I'm afraid. Afraid that I'll lose myself if I open up again."

He leaned closer, his voice soft but filled with conviction. "You won't lose yourself, Esmeray. You'll find yourself."

Their faces were inches apart, her breath mingling with his as her gaze searched his, looking for something, anything that could reassure her. Slowly, almost instinctively, she closed the distance between them, her lips brushing against his in a kiss that was both tentative and filled with a longing she could no longer deny.

The kiss deepened, slow and unhurried, as if savoring a moment they both knew was fragile and fleeting. Her fingers curled into his shirt, pulling him closer as his hands settled on her waist, holding her as if she might vanish. She was soft and warm against him, her barriers melting away as she allowed herself to feel, to surrender.

When they finally pulled apart, she looked at him, her eyes filled with a mixture of wonder and fear. "Darian… what are we doing?"

He smiled softly, his hand gently cupping her cheek. "We're breaking down walls. One crack at a time."

She let out a shaky laugh, her eyes glistening with unshed tears. "Then I hope you're prepared, dragon slayer. Because these walls are thick."

He pulled her close, his arms wrapping around her as he pressed a soft kiss to her forehead. "Then let them be thick. I'll be here, chipping away at them until there's nothing left but you, Esmeray. The woman behind the ice."

They sat together in the firelight, wrapped in each other's arms, letting the silence speak in ways that words couldn't. Esmeray rested her head against Darian's shoulder, her face partially hidden, yet she felt safe, sheltered by his warmth, his steady heartbeat beneath her cheek. Each beat seemed to whisper to her, telling her she wasn't alone, that she didn't have to bear the weight of her curse in silence. For the first time in what felt like centuries, she allowed herself to let go, if only a little, leaning into his embrace, savoring the comfort he offered so freely.

Darian's hand moved gently, tracing soft patterns along her arm, his touch tender and unhurried, as though he feared breaking the spell between them. He leaned his cheek against her hair, closing his eyes and breathing in the scent of her, a mix of cool night air and something indescribable that seemed uniquely hers. With each passing moment, the bond between them grew stronger, deeper, like the roots of an ancient tree breaking through frozen ground, seeking warmth and life.

"Esmeray," he murmured softly, breaking the silence, his voice a gentle caress in the dim light. She lifted her head, meeting his gaze, and he brushed a stray lock of hair behind her ear, his fingers lingering against her skin. "I meant what I said before. I'm here, and I'm not going anywhere."

Her eyes softened, and for the first time, she allowed herself to believe him, her hand reaching up to cover his. She leaned into his touch, letting herself get lost in the warmth of his gaze, feeling the last of her defenses waver. "I believe you," she whispered, her voice so quiet it was almost lost in the crackle of the fire. "I don't know why, but… I do."

He tilted her chin gently, his thumb brushing against her cheek. "Maybe because you've wanted to believe for a long time," he replied, his voice barely above a whisper.

Esmeray's heart ached at his words, as though he had laid bare a part of her that even she had been reluctant to acknowledge. Her eyes glistened, and she bit her lip, trying to hold back the tide of emotions she had long buried. But Darian's touch was too tender, too genuine, and before she knew it, a single tear slipped down her cheek.

He reached out, catching the tear with his thumb, his gaze softening as he looked at her with a reverence that made her breath hitch. "You don't have to hide from me, Esmeray," he whispered. "Not here, not now."

The vulnerability in his eyes, the sincerity in his words, unraveled her last defenses, and she allowed herself to surrender fully. She leaned into him, her hand moving to his chest, feeling the steady rhythm of his heartbeat beneath her palm. She looked up at him, her gaze filled with a mixture of fear and longing, and in that moment, she realized that she didn't want to push him away. She didn't want to be alone anymore.

With a tentative breath, she lifted her face, her lips brushing his in a soft, hesitant kiss. It was gentle, almost shy, as though testing the boundaries of this new, fragile connection between them. Darian's hand slid to the back of her neck, his fingers tangling in her hair as he deepened the kiss, his touch a silent promise that he was there, that he wouldn't let her fall.

Their kiss grew deeper, filled with a quiet passion that had been simmering between them, restrained but undeniable. His hand slipped around her waist, pulling her closer as if he were afraid she might disappear, as if he needed to anchor her to him. Her hands moved to his shoulders, gripping him as though he were her lifeline, grounding her in a way she hadn't felt in years.

"Darian…" she whispered against his lips, her voice trembling with emotion.

He pulled back slightly, his gaze searching hers. "What is it?"

She hesitated, struggling to find the words to express the turmoil within her. "I'm… afraid," she admitted, her voice barely above a whisper. "Afraid of letting myself feel this, afraid of what it might mean. I don't know if I can bear the pain of losing again."

Darian brushed a gentle kiss against her forehead, his arms wrapping around her more tightly. "Then don't think about losing," he whispered. "Think about now. Just this moment, you and me. Nothing else matters."

A soft sigh escaped her, and she nodded, allowing herself to sink into his embrace, to feel his warmth and strength surrounding her. They sat there in silence, wrapped in each other's arms, their breaths mingling, their hearts beating in time. Slowly, she felt the weight of her fears begin to melt away, replaced by a fragile hope she hadn't allowed herself to feel in centuries.

After a while, she lifted her head, her gaze meeting his with a newfound clarity. "Thank you," she murmured, her voice filled with a quiet gratitude that took him by surprise.

He smiled, brushing a tender hand along her cheek. "For what?"

"For… not giving up on me," she replied, her voice trembling with emotion. "For seeing past the ice, for believing that there's something worth saving."

Darian's expression softened, and he leaned down, pressing a gentle kiss to her forehead. "You are worth saving, Esmeray. You're worth everything."

She closed her eyes, letting his words sink into her, feeling the warmth of his love thaw the frozen parts of her heart. And as they held each other, wrapped in the glow of the firelight, she allowed herself to hope that maybe, just maybe, there was a future for them—a future filled with warmth, with love, with everything she had once thought was lost.

A Night of Secrets

Once again the following night the grand fire roared in the heart of the castle's hall, its golden light spilling across the icy walls and filling the room with warmth that defied the chill outside. Snow swept against the palace windows in thick, swirling gusts, but here, by the crackling fire, Darian and Esmeray sat alone, wrapped in a cocoon of warmth and quiet intimacy. Esmeray, who usually kept her distance, seemed more relaxed tonight, her posture less guarded, her gaze softened by the flickering firelight.

Darian shifted beside her, feeling the tension between them as if it were a living thing, something fragile and delicate, like a thread that could break at any moment. He watched her, noticing the way the shadows danced over her face, illuminating the slight furrow of her brow, the faint sadness that always seemed to linger just beneath her cool exterior. He wanted to reach out, to touch her hand and break the silence, but he sensed that tonight, Esmeray needed space to speak the truths that she kept so deeply hidden.

"It wasn't always like this," she began softly, her voice almost lost in the crackle of the flames. She didn't look at him, her gaze fixed on the fire, as if it held the answers to questions she hadn't asked in centuries.

"What wasn't?" he asked gently, his tone inviting her to continue, though he kept his distance, not wanting to intrude on her thoughts.

"This curse," she said, her voice thick with something he couldn't quite name. "The cold... the isolation. I wasn't always a queen shrouded in ice. Once, I was just... Esmeray. A woman who believed in love, in loyalty, in a future that I thought was certain."

Darian's heart ached at her words, the vulnerability in her tone stirring something deep within him. "What happened?" he asked softly, his gaze fixed on her as he leaned closer, sensing that she was finally allowing him a glimpse into the heart she kept so fiercely guarded.

She closed her eyes, taking a deep, shuddering breath before she continued. "I was betrayed. By someone I trusted with my life, my dreams, my heart." Her voice trembled slightly, her hand gripping the edge of her gown as though steadying herself. "His name was Alaric. He was a sorcerer, powerful and charming. When he came to my kingdom, he swept me off my feet, made me believe that he loved me, that he wanted to build a future with me."

Darian's fists clenched at his sides, a surge of anger rising in him at the thought of anyone hurting her. "And he didn't?" he asked, though he knew the answer was already written in the pain that clouded her gaze.

She shook her head, her lips curving into a bitter smile. "No. Alaric used me. He was after my kingdom's power, the ancient magic that flows through my bloodline. He manipulated my trust, made me fall in love with him, all so he could harness that power for himself. And once he had what he wanted... he left, abandoning me to the curse he had helped cast."

Darian felt a wave of fury at the thought of this man, Alaric, betraying her so cruelly. But he held himself in check, focusing on the woman beside him, the woman who, despite everything, had somehow managed to keep her heart intact, even if she hid it behind walls of ice. "I'm so sorry, Esmeray," he murmured, his voice thick with emotion. "No one deserves that."

She laughed softly, though there was no joy in the sound. "Perhaps I was naive," she said, her gaze distant. "I thought that love was something pure, something that could transcend power and ambition. But he taught me that love is nothing but a weakness, a weapon that can be turned against you when you least expect it."

Darian reached out, his hand covering hers in a gentle, reassuring gesture. She glanced down, surprise flickering across her face as if she hadn't expected the warmth of his touch. Her hand trembled slightly beneath his, and he gave her fingers a soft squeeze, silently telling her that he was there, that she didn't have to bear this burden alone.

"You are not defined by what he did to you, Esmeray," he said quietly, his voice steady and filled with conviction. "He may have tried to use you, to break you, but you're still here. You're still strong, still capable of feeling, even if you've tried to hide it."

She looked up at him, her eyes shimmering with unshed tears, her mask finally slipping away as she allowed herself to be seen. "But I'm afraid, Darian," she whispered, her voice trembling. "Afraid that if I let myself feel again, if I open my heart, I'll only be hurt. I can't bear the thought of being betrayed again, of being left alone."

He reached up, his thumb gently brushing a tear from her cheek, his touch soft and reverent. "I can't promise that I'll never hurt you, Esmeray. But I can promise that I'll never betray you. I'll be here, by your side, for as long as you'll let me."

Her breath hitched, her gaze searching his, as though trying to find some trace of deception, some sign that he was like Alaric. But all she saw was sincerity, a depth of feeling that left her breathless, vulnerable, and yet... hopeful.

"Why?" she murmured, her voice barely audible. "Why do you care so much, Darian? Why risk your life, your heart, for someone like me?"

He leaned closer, his forehead resting gently against hers, his voice a soft whisper. "Because I see you, Esmeray. I see the strength, the kindness, the love you still carry, even if you've buried it under layers of ice. And I can't help but want to know the woman behind the queen, the heart behind the curse."

A tear slipped down her cheek, and she closed her eyes, allowing herself to surrender to the warmth of his presence, to the feeling that maybe, just maybe, she didn't have to face this life alone. His arms wrapped around her, pulling her close, and she let herself lean into him, her head resting against his chest as she listened to the steady beat of his heart, a sound that grounded her, soothed her in ways she hadn't thought possible.

After a long moment, she lifted her head, her gaze meeting his with a mixture of fear and longing. "I don't know if I can do this, Darian," she whispered, her voice trembling. "I've been alone for so long, held myself back for so long. I'm afraid I'll never be able to let go."

He cupped her face in his hands, his thumbs brushing gently over her cheeks as he looked into her eyes, his gaze filled with a quiet, unyielding determination. "Then let me be the one to break down those walls," he murmured, his voice a gentle plea. "One crack at a time. Let me show you that love doesn't have to be a weapon. It can be something beautiful, something worth fighting for."

Her breath shuddered, and she leaned into his touch, her eyes fluttering closed as he lowered his lips to hers, their mouths meeting in a kiss that was soft and tender, filled with a vulnerability that took her breath away. His hands slid down to her waist, pulling her closer as she wrapped her arms around his neck, allowing herself to lose herself in his warmth, in the safety of his embrace.

Their kiss deepened, slow and unhurried, as though savoring a moment that felt both fragile and eternal. She felt the ice around her heart begin to melt, felt the warmth of his love seeping into the parts of her she had kept locked away, hidden from the world. His touch was gentle, reverent, as though he were afraid to break her, to shatter the delicate trust they had built.

When they finally pulled apart, their foreheads rested together, their breaths mingling in the firelight as they looked at each other, their eyes filled with a mixture of fear and hope, of promises unspoken yet deeply felt.

"Stay with me, Darian," she whispered, her voice barely audible. "I don't know what the future holds, but… I want you here, with me."

He smiled, pressing a soft kiss to her forehead. "I'm not going anywhere, Esmeray," he murmured, his voice filled with quiet conviction. "I'll be here, by your side, for as long as you'll have me."

They held each other in the firelight, wrapped in a warmth that defied the chill of the castle, of the curse that had bound her for centuries. And in that moment, as they sat together, hearts intertwined, Esmeray felt something she hadn't felt in years—a fragile hope, a glimmer of love that promised to thaw the frozen parts of her soul, one tender moment at a time.

The Heart of the Ice Dragon

The dawn broke over the icy mountains, casting a pale light over the castle. Darian wandered through the halls, his mind filled with the weight of the night before—the tender moments he'd shared with Esmeray, the vulnerability she had shown him. He felt himself drawn deeper into her world, pulled in by something he couldn't explain, a force that seemed beyond duty or reason.

But as much as they had connected, he knew there were still secrets, still pieces of her heart she held back, guarded by walls of ice. And he wanted—no, he needed—to understand her curse fully if he ever hoped to help her. Yet Esmeray had shut down every time he came close to the truth, as if some part of her refused to hope, refused to believe that she might find a way out.

Lost in thought, he nearly collided with Thorian, Esmeray's advisor, who was pacing the hallway with a scroll in his hands, his expression thoughtful. Thorian's dark eyes glanced up, a flicker of surprise crossing his face as he noticed Darian.

"Ah, the dragon slayer," Thorian remarked, his tone both amused and wary. "Or should I say... the queen's guest?" His gaze sharpened as he looked Darian over, as if assessing his intentions.

Darian nodded, a faint smile touching his lips. "I suppose either title works," he replied, though his tone was thoughtful. "Though I don't feel much like a dragon slayer here."

"Is that so?" Thorian arched a brow, a hint of curiosity in his gaze. "I'd think it would take quite a bit for a man trained to kill dragons to find himself... softened by one."

Darian held Thorian's gaze, his expression resolute. "Esmeray is much more than the dragon she becomes, and I think you know that as well as I do."

Thorian's eyes darkened slightly, though he nodded. "Yes, she is much more. But that 'more' is also what makes her curse so difficult to break." He sighed, folding the scroll and tucking it under his arm. "The magic that binds her is no ordinary spell. It's tied to her very heart, to the love she once held but was betrayed by. And she has buried that love deep, where even she can't reach it."

Darian's interest piqued, and he took a step closer. "What do you mean? I know her heart was broken, that someone she trusted betrayed her, but how does that connect to the curse?"

Thorian's gaze softened, a mixture of sadness and understanding in his eyes. "Her heart is quite literally frozen, encased in ice by the magic of the curse. Alaric, the man who betrayed her, bound her power to her broken heart, cursing her to live half her life as a dragon and the other as a queen, forever denied love and warmth. To break the curse, she would need to experience true love—love that would melt the ice around her heart."

Darian's chest tightened, the weight of Thorian's words settling over him. "She doesn't believe in love," he said quietly, his voice filled with both sorrow and frustration. "She's convinced herself that love is dangerous, that it only brings pain."

Thorian nodded, his expression weary. "And can you blame her? She has lived with this curse for centuries, watched friends and family grow old and die, while she remains trapped in a cycle of isolation. She's built walls around her heart so high that even she can no longer see over them."

Darian clenched his fists, feeling a surge of determination. "Then I'll climb those walls if I have to. I don't care how long it takes—I'll prove to her that love isn't a weakness."

Thorian's eyes softened, a faint smile curving his lips. "Perhaps you're exactly what she needs, Darian. Just… be careful. Esmeray's heart is fragile, and any hint of betrayal, real or perceived, will only make her retreat further into the ice."

Darian nodded, his resolve firm. "I understand."

Later that evening, Darian found Esmeray in the grand hall, standing before a large tapestry that depicted the history of her kingdom. She looked ethereal in the glow of the torchlight, her gaze distant, lost in thought. He approached her slowly, and she turned at the sound of his footsteps, a guarded expression flickering across her face.

"Darian," she greeted him softly, a hint of warmth in her eyes that quickly faded. "I didn't expect to see you tonight."

"I wanted to spend some time with you," he said, his voice gentle, as he came to stand beside her. "I wanted to know more… about your curse."

Her gaze hardened, and she turned away, her arms crossing over her chest. "Why do you keep asking?" she murmured, her voice laced with frustration. "My curse is just that—a curse. A punishment I carry alone."

"Maybe you don't have to carry it alone," he replied, his voice steady. "Maybe there's a way to break it."

Esmeray laughed, though there was no humor in the sound. "Break it? And how do you propose to do that, Darian? Magic? A sword? Some whispered promise of hope?" She shook her head, her eyes cold. "My heart is frozen, buried beneath centuries of ice. Love, as you may have guessed, is not something I believe in anymore."

He reached out, his hand gently resting on her shoulder, his touch warm against the chill that surrounded her. "I believe in it," he said softly, his gaze unwavering. "And I believe that maybe, somewhere deep down, you still do too."

Her breath hitched, and she looked up at him, her eyes filled with a mixture of anger and something else, something fragile and uncertain. "Darian, don't," she whispered, her voice trembling. "You don't know what you're saying. This curse is not something you can break with words."

"Then let me try," he murmured, his hand slipping down to cover hers. "Let me try to show you that love doesn't have to hurt."

She pulled her hand back, her gaze steeling as she took a step away from him. "You're a fool," she said, though her voice wavered. "A fool who sees only what he wants to see."

He held her gaze, refusing to back down. "Maybe I am a fool. But I'd rather be a fool who believes in love than someone who hides from it."

Esmeray turned away, her shoulders tense, her hands clenched at her sides. "Darian... even if you could break through, even if you could make me believe again... it won't change what I am. I am bound to this kingdom, to this curse. You can't save me from myself."

He stepped closer, his voice filled with quiet determination. "I don't need to save you, Esmeray. I just want to be with you, to show you that there's more to life than this curse."

She looked at him, her expression softening, and for a moment, he thought she might let him in. But then her gaze flickered past him, and her face hardened as she straightened, her queenly mask slipping back into place.

"Your intentions are noble, Darian," she said, her tone cool. "But I cannot allow myself to hope for something that will only bring more pain."

Before he could respond, Thorian entered the hall, his expression serious as he approached them. He glanced between them, his gaze lingering on Esmeray before he spoke.

"Your Majesty, forgive the interruption," he said, his tone respectful yet firm. "But there is news from the southern border. The other kingdoms are growing restless. They sense a weakness in our defenses."

Esmeray's posture stiffened, her gaze turning cold as she regarded Thorian. "Then we will remind them of our strength," she replied, her tone hard. "Send word to the generals. I want our forces doubled at the border."

Thorian nodded, his gaze flickering to Darian before he turned back to Esmeray. "Of course, Your

Majesty. But... perhaps it would be wise to consider another option."

Esmeray's gaze narrowed. "What are you suggesting?"

Thorian hesitated, glancing at Darian before he spoke. "Perhaps an alliance. There are those who would stand with us, who would see our kingdom as a friend rather than an enemy."

Esmeray's eyes flashed with anger. "An alliance? With those who would seek to control us? I think not."

Darian stepped forward, his voice calm but firm. "Maybe Thorian is right, Esmeray. Maybe there's another way to protect your people, a way that doesn't involve more walls, more isolation."

She looked at him, her expression a mixture of frustration and sorrow. "You don't understand, Darian. I have protected this kingdom alone for centuries. I can't allow myself to trust others, to rely on promises that could be broken."

He reached out, his hand gently cupping her face, his thumb brushing over her cheek. "Then trust me," he murmured, his voice filled with a quiet plea. "Trust that I won't leave you, that I won't betray you. Let me be the one who stands by your side."

For a long moment, she looked at him, her gaze filled with a depth of emotion she could no longer hide. Slowly, she lifted her hand, her fingers brushing over his, her touch hesitant but filled with a quiet yearning.

"Darian..." she whispered, her voice filled with both fear and longing. "If I let myself hope... if I let myself believe... what then?"

"Then we'll face it together," he replied, his voice steady, his gaze unwavering. "One step at a time."

She closed her eyes, leaning into his touch, allowing herself to feel the warmth of his hand, the strength of his presence. And in that moment, as they stood together by the fire, the ice around her heart cracked, if only slightly, letting in a warmth she hadn't allowed herself to feel in centuries.

Thorian, watching them from a distance, allowed himself a faint smile, a glimmer of hope that maybe, just maybe, this dragon slayer could be the one to break the curse that had bound his queen for so long.

The Attack

The peaceful quiet of the evening was shattered by the piercing screech of dragons echoing through the cold, dark sky. Darian jerked awake, adrenaline instantly flooding his system as he bolted upright, his hand instinctively reaching for his sword. He could hear the frantic footsteps of soldiers rushing through the halls, the clang of armor, and the shouts of alarm filling the castle.

A shadow appeared in his doorway, and he turned to see Thorian, his face grim and urgent.

"We're under attack," Thorian said, his voice steady but laced with tension. "Rival dragons from the southern lands. They sense the Ice Queen's weakening power."

Darian's heart pounded as he strapped his sword to his waist. "Where's Esmeray?"

"She's already outside, in her dragon form," Thorian replied, his eyes darkening. "But they're more organized than we anticipated. There's a powerful sorcerer among them, controlling the dragons and other creatures. She can't do this alone."

Darian gave Thorian a firm nod and raced down the corridors, his thoughts focused solely on Esmeray. As he reached the main gates, he pushed his way through the soldiers, emerging onto the icy field outside the castle just in time to see Esmeray's dragon form battling two enormous rival dragons, her silvery scales flashing like a storm in the night. She let out a furious roar, her tail lashing as she tore into one of her attackers with fierce, calculated strikes.

But even as she fought, Darian could see the strain on her, the way her movements had lost a bit of their usual precision, the exhaustion that dulled her once-sharp strikes.

He tightened his grip on his sword and charged forward, joining the fray, weaving his way through the chaos. Creatures he'd only heard of in legends—a massive wyvern, frost-breathing wolves, and shadowy figures that moved faster than human eyes could follow—clashed with Esmeray's soldiers. With swift, practiced moves, Darian slashed through the creatures, cutting down anything that dared stand in his way.

"Esmeray!" he shouted, trying to get her attention as he fought his way toward her.

She turned, her dragon eyes meeting his, and he saw the mixture of relief and fear in her gaze. But before she could respond, another dragon lunged at her, jaws wide as it went for her throat. Darian felt his heart skip a beat, but Esmeray twisted, her massive form moving with surprising agility as she sank her teeth into her attacker's neck, throwing it to the ground with a mighty crash.

Darian fought his way closer to her, his sword flashing as he cut through the oncoming wave of creatures. A frost wolf lunged at him, its breath a cloud of icy mist, and he sidestepped, driving his blade deep into its chest before spinning to block the swipe of a wyvern's talons. His movements were fluid, precise, each strike calculated and efficient. But no matter how many he felled, there seemed to be no end to the onslaught.

Above him, Esmeray was locked in a brutal fight with a particularly large and aggressive dragon, its scales a dark, stormy gray. She was powerful, her strikes ferocious, but Darian could see the toll it was taking on her. Her wings faltered for a brief moment, and the gray dragon took advantage, sinking its claws into her shoulder.

"No!" Darian shouted, fear gripping his heart as he saw her stumble.

Gathering every ounce of strength, Esmeray shook the dragon off, retaliating with a fierce blast of icy breath that drove her opponent back. But Darian knew she couldn't keep this up alone. The rival dragons were relentless, and without help, she'd be overwhelmed.

With grim determination, he fought his way to her side, finally breaking through the ranks of creatures. He glanced up at her, shouting over the chaos.

"Esmeray! Let me help!"

She roared in response, the sound filled with frustration and fury, but she didn't reject his offer. Instead, she took a defensive stance, positioning herself so that Darian could cover her weaker side. Together, they fought in sync, each one protecting the other, a seamless dance of sword and claw.

As they battled side by side, Darian noticed a figure cloaked in dark robes standing atop a nearby ridge, a staff raised, directing the chaos below. The sorcerer. This was the puppet master, the one controlling the rival dragons and creatures.

"Esmeray!" he shouted, pointing toward the figure. "He's the one behind this! We need to take him out!"

Her dragon eyes followed his gaze, narrowing as she saw the sorcerer. She gave a fierce nod, her massive form shifting as she prepared to charge. But before she could take flight, two more dragons descended, blocking her path.

"Go!" Darian shouted. "I'll handle them!"

She hesitated for a brief moment, her eyes meeting his, a mixture of fear and gratitude in her gaze. Then, with a powerful beat of her wings, she took off, soaring toward the sorcerer as Darian squared off against the dragons.

The battle was fierce, each strike pushing Darian closer to his limits, but he fought with everything he had, knowing that Esmeray was counting on him. The first dragon lunged, its jaws snapping inches from his face, and he rolled to the side, his sword flashing as he drove it deep into its side. It let out a furious roar, thrashing as it tried to shake him off, but he held firm, twisting the blade until the dragon fell with a final, shuddering breath.

The second dragon was on him before he had time to recover, its massive tail lashing out and sending him sprawling. His vision blurred, pain radiating through his body as he struggled to his feet, gripping his sword tightly. But before the dragon could strike again, a blast of icy breath swept over it, freezing it in place. Darian looked up to see Esmeray, back at his side, her dragon eyes fierce as she protected him.

"You came back," he murmured, a mixture of relief and awe in his voice.

She shifted back to her human form, breathing heavily as she knelt beside him, her hand reaching out to brush a strand of hair from his face. "I couldn't let you face them alone," she whispered, her voice filled with emotion. "Not when you've fought so hard to stand by me."

He took her hand, his grip firm and reassuring. "Esmeray, you can't do this alone anymore. I know you're strong, but even the strongest need someone by their side."

Her gaze softened, a hint of vulnerability shining through her usual stoic expression. "You don't understand, Darian. This kingdom, this curse... I was meant to bear it alone. I can't let anyone else shoulder that burden."

He shook his head, his eyes filled with determination. "You're wrong. This isn't just your fight anymore. I'm here, Esmeray. I'm not going to let you face this alone."

Her breath hitched, and she looked at him with a mixture of fear and hope, as if daring to believe him. "But what if I lose you?" she whispered, her voice barely audible. "What if... what if loving you only brings more pain?"

He reached up, his hand gently cupping her cheek, his thumb brushing away a stray tear. "Then we face that together. You've been alone for so long, Esmeray. Let me be the one to help you carry this. Let me be the one to melt the ice around your heart."

A tear slipped down her cheek, and she leaned into his touch, her eyes closing as she allowed herself to feel, to hope. "Darian... I don't know if I can love again," she murmured, her voice filled with both fear and longing.

He smiled softly, his hand moving to the back of her neck as he pulled her close. "Then let me show you how."

Their lips met in a kiss that was both fierce and tender, a collision of fire and ice that spoke of promises and vulnerabilities, of a love that was still fragile but growing stronger with every moment. The world around them faded, the battle forgotten as they clung to each other, each one finding solace in the other's warmth.

When they finally pulled apart, her gaze was filled with a newfound determination, her hand gripping his tightly. "Together," she murmured, her voice steady. "We face this together."

They rose to their feet, turning to face the remaining enemies, their strength bolstered by the bond they had forged, a bond that went beyond duty, beyond the curse, beyond anything either of them had known before. And as they stood side by side, the firelight glinting off their forms, Darian knew that this was only the beginning—that together, they could face anything the world threw at them.

And perhaps, just perhaps, they could finally break the curse that had bound her heart for so long.

The Fire Within

The battle had ended, but the echoes of it still lingered, hanging over the castle like a ghostly mist. The halls were filled with weary soldiers tending to wounds and quietly recounting the events of the night. Darian moved through the stone corridors, his own bruises aching but his thoughts fixated on Esmeray. After the night's chaos, he needed to see her, to know she was all right.

He found her on the balcony overlooking the mountains, her figure silhouetted against the twilight. She seemed lost in thought, her posture tense as if she were holding onto some invisible weight. Darian approached slowly, the soft sound of his boots on the stone floor catching her attention. She turned, her expression softening as her gaze met his, though he could see the turmoil simmering beneath the surface.

"You're safe," he murmured, his voice filled with relief as he stopped beside her.

She offered him a small smile, but her eyes were distant, haunted. "Thanks to you," she replied softly. "You fought bravely, Darian. I didn't think… I didn't expect you to risk so much."

He reached out, his hand brushing against hers, a gentle touch that felt both reassuring and grounding. "I'd do it again. For you, for this kingdom." He hesitated, his gaze intense. "You don't have to be alone anymore, Esmeray."

Her gaze dropped to their hands, her fingers curling instinctively around his before she caught herself, pulling back as if his touch burned her. She turned away, gripping the stone railing as she looked out over the mountains, her expression conflicted.

"It's not that simple," she whispered, her voice barely audible. "I... I want to believe you, Darian. But I've been down this path before, and all it brought me was pain. Betrayal. I can't risk my heart again."

He stepped closer, his voice gentle but firm. "Esmeray, I'm not him. I'm not Alaric. I would never betray you."

Her shoulders tensed, and she looked back at him, her eyes flashing with a mixture of anger and sorrow. "You don't understand, Darian. It's not just about trust. It's about the curse, the power that binds me. My heart... it was literally frozen, locked away to protect me, but it has kept me isolated, unable to truly feel."

Darian reached out again, his hand covering hers on the railing, his warmth seeping into her skin. "And yet here you are, feeling. I've seen it, Esmeray. I've seen the way you care, the way you fought to protect this kingdom. You may try to hide it, but there's a fire within you, a warmth that you've buried beneath the ice."

She looked down, her defenses weakening as his words stirred something deep within her. "Darian, I can't," she murmured, her voice trembling. "I've lived with this curse for so long. Opening myself to… this, to you… it terrifies me."

He stepped closer, his other hand coming up to gently tilt her face toward him, his gaze soft and unwavering. "It's all right to be afraid," he said quietly. "I'm afraid too. But sometimes, the only way to break free is to let someone in, to let them help carry the weight."

Her eyes filled with unshed tears, her voice breaking. "But what if I lose you? What if… what if this ends in nothing but pain?"

Darian leaned in, his forehead resting gently against hers, their breaths mingling in the cool night air. "Then we'll face that together. But I'm willing to risk it, Esmeray, if it means even a chance of truly being with you."

A tear slipped down her cheek, and he brushed it away with his thumb, his touch soft and tender. For a long moment, she simply looked at him, her heart pounding as she let herself feel the warmth of his presence, the comfort he offered so freely. Her walls, the ones she had fortified over centuries, were crumbling, and as terrifying as it was, she found herself wanting to let them fall.

With a shaky breath, she looked up at him, her voice barely a whisper. "I don't know if I can love again, Darian. I don't know if I'm even capable of it."

He smiled, a gentle, understanding smile that made her heart ache. "Then let me show you," he murmured, his lips brushing softly over hers. It was a tentative, unhurried kiss, filled with a tenderness that took her breath away. She found herself leaning into him, her hands gripping his shoulders as if he were an anchor, grounding her, reminding her that she didn't have to face her fears alone.

Their kiss deepened, slow and unhurried, as though savoring a moment they both knew was fragile and precious. His arms wrapped around her, pulling her close, and she let herself melt into him, feeling the warmth of his embrace seep into the frozen parts of her heart. For the first time in centuries, she allowed herself to feel—to truly feel.

When they finally pulled apart, she looked up at him, her gaze filled with a mixture of awe and fear. "Darian… this is dangerous," she whispered, her voice trembling.

"Love often is," he replied, his fingers brushing a stray lock of hair behind her ear. "But sometimes, it's worth the risk."

She closed her eyes, leaning into his touch, her mind a whirlwind of emotions. Her heart, the one she'd thought was frozen beyond repair, was stirring, waking up to the possibility of love, of warmth, of a future she'd long since given up on.

But just as she was about to speak, they heard footsteps approaching, and she reluctantly stepped back, her mask slipping back into place as Thorian appeared, his expression neutral but his eyes knowing.

"Forgive me for interrupting," Thorian said, though his tone suggested he knew exactly what he was interrupting. "But there are matters that require your attention, Your Majesty."

Esmeray nodded, her expression guarded once more, though Darian could see the hint of vulnerability lingering in her gaze. "Of course, Thorian. I'll be there shortly."

Thorian inclined his head, casting a quick glance at Darian before he turned and walked away. Darian watched him go, sensing that the advisor understood more than he let on. He turned back to Esmeray, his hand reaching out to take hers.

"Esmeray," he murmured, his voice filled with quiet determination. "Don't shut me out. Not now."

She looked down at their joined hands, her heart pounding as she fought against the fear that gnawed at her, the voice that told her this was too dangerous, that love would only bring her pain. But as she looked into his eyes, the warmth and sincerity in his gaze chipped away at her defenses.

"I... I don't know how to do this," she admitted, her voice barely above a whisper. "I don't know how to let someone in after everything I've been through."

He smiled, his thumb gently stroking her hand. "Then let me show you. One day at a time."

A faint smile tugged at her lips, and she nodded, allowing herself a glimmer of hope. "All right," she whispered, her voice soft but resolute. "One day at a time."

They stood together in silence, the night air cool around them, the warmth of their connection a quiet promise in the darkness. And as they held each other, Esmeray felt the fire within her grow stronger, melting away the ice that had kept her heart locked away for so long. For the first time, she dared to believe that maybe, just maybe, she could find a way to love again.

The Thawing Heart

Days drifted into nights, and the castle, once echoing with silence and cold, began to feel warmer, more alive. Esmeray found herself seeking Darian out without realizing it, her once solitary routine now punctuated by shared glances, soft words, and the comfort of his presence. He was there in quiet moments, standing beside her in the great hall as they discussed the kingdom's defense, or simply walking with her through the castle gardens, the frost-covered roses glistening in the evening light.

For the first time in centuries, Esmeray felt her heart begin to thaw, warmth creeping into the cracks that Darian had slowly, patiently widened. And yet, the closer she grew to him, the more she feared the intensity of her feelings.

One evening, they stood together on the balcony, watching the last of the sunlight slip beneath the horizon. The sky was a wash of indigo and gold, a perfect reflection of the magic she could feel simmering between them. Darian stood close, his gaze on the view, but she sensed his awareness of her, the slight shift of his posture as if he was waiting, hoping.

"Your kingdom is beautiful in the evening," he murmured, breaking the silence.

Esmeray nodded, her voice soft. "It wasn't always this way. Once, before the curse, it was filled with life and laughter. The halls echoed with music. Now... it feels like it's frozen in time, like I am."

Darian turned to her, his expression thoughtful. "I don't think you're frozen, Esmeray," he said, his voice gentle. "You're just... guarded. You've been hurt, and you built walls to keep others out. But that doesn't mean your heart isn't still beating, still wanting to be whole."

She looked away, her fingers gripping the stone railing as she wrestled with the truth of his words. "Sometimes, I wonder if it's easier to stay hidden, to keep everyone at a distance. Caring for someone... it only opens you up to pain."

"Or to joy," he replied, stepping closer, his gaze never leaving her face. "You can't have one without the other. And I think, deep down, you know that. You've just been afraid to let yourself feel again."

Esmeray's breath caught, her heart pounding as she felt his warmth so close beside her, his words cutting through her defenses. She looked up at him, her eyes filled with a mixture of fear and longing, emotions she hadn't allowed herself to feel in centuries.

"Darian," she murmured, her voice trembling. "I don't know if I can..."

"Then don't think," he whispered, his hand gently cupping her cheek, his thumb brushing over her skin. "Just feel."

She closed her eyes, surrendering to his touch, to the quiet intensity that filled the space between them. His hand slid to the back of her neck, and he leaned in, his lips meeting hers in a kiss that was tender and unhurried, filled with a longing that took her breath away. She melted against him, her hands moving to his shoulders, gripping him as if he were her anchor, grounding her in a storm of emotions she could no longer deny.

The kiss deepened, filled with a fierce, unspoken need, the years of solitude and heartbreak fading away as she allowed herself to feel the warmth of his embrace, the strength of his love. He pulled her closer, his hands gentle yet possessive, as though he were afraid to let her go. And for a moment, she let herself believe that this could be real, that maybe, just maybe, she could have a future free from the curse, from the loneliness.

But as the kiss lingered, a flicker of fear surfaced, cold and sharp, reminding her of the pain she had endured, of the betrayal that had left her heart shattered and encased in ice. She pulled back, her gaze filled with confusion and fear as she looked up at him, her heart racing.

"I can't," she whispered, stepping back, her hand pressed against her chest as if to still the frantic beat of her heart. "Darian, I... I'm not sure I can do this."

He looked at her, hurt flickering across his face, though he quickly masked it, his expression softening as he reached for her hand. "Esmeray," he said quietly, his voice filled with understanding. "It's all right to be afraid. But I know there's more to you than this curse, this fear. I see the woman behind the ice, and I know she's worth fighting for."

She shook her head, pulling her hand from his grasp, her eyes filled with a sorrow she couldn't contain. "You don't understand. Loving someone... it opens you up to weakness, to betrayal. I can't afford to let myself feel that again. I can't risk my heart, not after everything I've endured."

Darian took a step closer, his voice steady, unwavering. "You're stronger than you think, Esmeray. You've survived betrayal, heartbreak, and centuries of solitude. But you're not living—you're just surviving. Letting yourself love doesn't make you weak. It makes you brave."

She looked away, her hands trembling as she gripped the edge of the balcony, her heart a storm of conflicting emotions. "I don't know if I can be brave, Darian. Not like you. I've spent so long convincing myself that love is a weakness, that it only brings pain. I don't know how to see it any other way."

He reached out, his hand covering hers on the railing, his touch warm and grounding. "Then let me show you. Let me be the one to stand beside you, to help you see that love doesn't have to be a curse. That it can be… a new beginning."

Her breath hitched, and she looked up at him, her gaze filled with a mixture of hope and fear. "But what if it ends in pain?" she whispered, her voice barely audible. "What if… what if I lose you?"

He smiled, his gaze filled with a quiet, unyielding determination. "Then we face that together. Life is full of risks, Esmeray. But I'm willing to take that risk if it means a chance with you."

A tear slipped down her cheek, and she closed her eyes, allowing herself to lean into his touch, to feel the warmth of his hand against hers. "I don't know if I'm ready," she admitted, her voice a trembling whisper.

He leaned in, pressing a soft, gentle kiss to her forehead. "Then take your time," he murmured. "I'm not going anywhere."

They stood in silence, wrapped in each other's presence, the warmth of his embrace a quiet promise in the darkness. She let herself relax against him, feeling the steady beat of his heart, the strength of his love, a love that was patient and unwavering.

After a long moment, she looked up at him, her gaze filled with a fragile hope. "I... I want to try," she whispered, her voice barely above a breath. "I don't know if I can do this, but... I want to try."

He smiled, his hand gently cupping her cheek as he looked into her eyes. "That's all I ask."

The world around them seemed to fall away as Esmeray felt herself drawn deeper into Darian's embrace, her walls crumbling with each beat of her heart. His hand moved slowly, reverently, brushing a strand of hair from her face as he gazed into her eyes, his expression filled with warmth and something so pure it took her breath away. Her pulse quickened as she held his gaze, feeling vulnerable yet safe, as though his arms were the only place she was meant to be.

"Esmeray," he murmured, his voice a soft caress that sent a shiver down her spine. He tilted her chin, his hand resting gently on the back of her neck, and she felt her breath hitch as he leaned in, their lips mere inches apart. "I need you to know... whatever lies ahead, I'm here with you. For you."

She closed her eyes, her heart pounding as she felt his lips brush against hers, the kiss tender and exploratory, a whisper of what lay beneath their restraint. But as he deepened the kiss, her resolve melted, and she allowed herself to fall into the moment, to surrender to the passion that had simmered between them for so long. Her hands slid up his chest, gripping the fabric of his shirt as if to hold onto the reality of him, her anchor amid the storm of emotions she'd suppressed for centuries.

Their kiss grew more fervent, filled with the unspoken longing and desire that had built between them, both of them giving in to the intensity of what they felt, no longer restrained by fear or hesitation. His hands moved to her waist, pulling her closer as if he couldn't bear to have any distance between them, and she responded in kind, her own hands finding their way to the back of his neck, fingers threading through his hair.

"Darian," she whispered against his lips, her voice trembling with both passion and vulnerability. She could feel the warmth of his breath, the steady rhythm of his heartbeat, grounding her, assuring her that this was real, that he was here. He kissed her again, deeper this time, pouring every unspoken promise into the embrace, each kiss a declaration that words could never capture.

They stood together in the cool night air, her body pressed against his, the warmth between them a stark contrast to the chill that had once defined her life. His hands were strong yet gentle, his touch filled with a tenderness that left her feeling cherished, desired. She felt herself melting, the icy defenses she'd built around her heart finally giving way to the fire he had sparked within her.

When they finally pulled apart, both breathless, Darian rested his forehead against hers, their eyes meeting in a silent exchange that said more than words ever could. His thumb brushed gently across her cheek, his gaze filled with a love so fierce and unyielding that it made her heart ache in a way that was both beautiful and terrifying.

"You're worth every risk," he whispered, his voice a promise that settled deep within her, anchoring her in ways she hadn't known she needed. "And I'm not going anywhere."

She let out a shaky breath, her eyes glistening as she smiled, her fingers tracing the line of his jaw. "Then neither am I," she murmured, her voice soft but resolute, the words carrying the weight of a vow, a promise to finally let herself live, to love.

They stood together in the embrace of the night, holding each other as if the world beyond the balcony didn't exist, as if this moment could last forever. And as they held each other, their hearts beating in sync, Esmeray felt the last of her fears slip away, replaced by a warmth that filled her from within, a fire that promised not only a new beginning but a love that would endure, strong and true, against all odds.

The Ice Queen's Dilemma

The next morning, Esmeray found herself pacing the grand hall, her mind a storm of emotions that she could no longer ignore. The intensity of her feelings for Darian scared her. She had long mastered the art of locking her emotions away, of keeping her heart cold and unreachable. But with him, every defense, every wall she had built felt fragile, ready to collapse at the slightest touch.

Their kiss the night before had awakened something within her that she had thought long dead. She felt alive, more alive than she had in centuries, and yet, the vulnerability that came with it was overwhelming. Every time she closed her eyes, she could feel the warmth of his hands on her waist, the steadiness of his gaze as he promised not to leave. Her heart ached with longing, but there was a whisper of fear that told her to keep her distance, to protect herself.

The sound of approaching footsteps drew her attention, and she turned to see Darian entering the hall, his expression softening when he saw her. His presence filled the room with a calm warmth, a stark contrast to the turmoil inside her. Esmeray's pulse quickened, and she fought the urge to turn away, to shield herself from the emotions his gaze stirred.

"Esmeray," he said, his voice gentle as he approached her. "You've been avoiding me."

She took a step back, her posture stiffening as she tried to regain her composure. "I have responsibilities, Darian. A kingdom to protect. I can't afford distractions."

His brow furrowed, his gaze searching hers. "You think that's what this is? A distraction?"

She averted her eyes, unable to hold his gaze. "I think that... I have allowed myself to grow careless, to let my emotions cloud my judgment. This... whatever it is between us... it cannot continue. I cannot afford to let my heart lead me astray."

Darian sighed, his expression a mixture of frustration and understanding. "Esmeray, you're not leading yourself astray. You're protecting yourself from something you've wanted for a long time, and I think you know that."

She clenched her fists, anger flaring as she looked up at him, her voice sharp. "You don't understand, Darian. You don't know what it's like to bear the weight of this kingdom alone, to face the betrayal and pain that I have endured. Love is a weakness, a vulnerability I cannot afford."

He took a step closer, his gaze unwavering. "Love isn't a weakness. It's what gives us strength. It's what makes us human, what makes us fight for what matters. Don't you see? By shutting yourself off from love, from the people who care about you, you're only weakening yourself."

Her heart ached at his words, but she shook her head, her voice trembling. "I am not like you, Darian. I cannot simply open my heart and hope for the best. I have seen what love can do. It blinds, it betrays. It leaves you broken."

Darian's expression softened, his eyes filled with a tenderness that made her heart ache. "Esmeray, I am not Alaric," he said quietly. "I'm not here to hurt you, to take anything from you. I'm here because I care about you, because I believe in the woman behind the ice, the woman who deserves to be loved."

She felt her defenses crumbling, the weight of his words settling over her, but she forced herself to remain firm, to keep her emotions in check. "You may think that now," she said, her voice barely above a whisper. "But love is fleeting, Darian. People change. They grow tired, they leave. It's easier, safer, to remain alone."

Darian took another step toward her, his hand reaching out to gently touch her arm, grounding her in a way she hadn't expected. "Is that what you truly want? A life without connection, without love? A life of isolation?" His gaze softened, and his voice dropped to a gentle murmur. "Or are you just afraid of letting yourself feel?"

She looked up at him, her throat tightening as she fought against the vulnerability his words stirred within her. "I am afraid," she admitted, her voice breaking. "I'm terrified, Darian. Because if I allow myself to love you… and if I lose you… I don't think I could survive it."

He stepped closer, his hand moving to cup her cheek, his touch warm and reassuring. "Then let me be here. Let me be the one who doesn't leave, who doesn't betray. You've been carrying this weight alone for too long, Esmeray. You don't have to bear it all on your own."

Her breath hitched, and she felt herself leaning into his touch, her heart pounding as his words resonated within her. She wanted to believe him, wanted to believe that love didn't have to be painful, that it could be a source of strength. But the fear lingered, whispering that this happiness, this warmth, was something she didn't deserve, something that would only end in pain.

"Darian," she murmured, her voice trembling. "I don't know if I can do this. I don't know if I can open myself up again."

He leaned in, his forehead resting against hers as he spoke softly, his voice filled with quiet conviction. "You don't have to know everything right now. Just take it one day at a time. Let yourself feel, let yourself believe that you're worth this, that you're worth being loved."

A tear slipped down her cheek, and he brushed it away with his thumb, his gaze tender as he looked into her eyes. "Esmeray, I'm not going anywhere. I'll be here, for as long as you'll have me."

For a long moment, she stood there, her heart racing as she let his words sink in, let herself believe that maybe, just maybe, he was telling the truth. She reached up, her hand covering his as she leaned into him, her resolve crumbling as the walls around her heart began to fall.

Without another word, she closed the distance between them, her lips meeting his in a kiss that was filled with both fear and longing, a desperate need to be held, to be loved. He responded immediately, his arms wrapping around her, pulling her close as he deepened the kiss, his touch filled with a tenderness that took her breath away.

Her hands found their way to the back of his neck, pulling him closer as she surrendered to the warmth, to the passion that had been building between them. Each kiss, each touch, was a reassurance, a silent promise that he would be there, that he wouldn't leave her. She felt the ice within her melt, the cold fear that had kept her heart locked away fading in the warmth of his embrace.

When they finally pulled apart, they were both breathless, their foreheads pressed together as they gazed into each other's eyes, a quiet understanding passing between them.

"Stay with me," she whispered, her voice barely audible, her hand still resting on his cheek. "I don't know what the future holds, but… I don't want to face it alone."

He smiled, pressing a soft kiss to her forehead. "I'm not going anywhere, Esmeray," he murmured. "I'll be by your side, for as long as you'll have me."

They held each other in the quiet of the hall, the warmth between them a stark contrast to the icy walls that surrounded them. And for the first time in centuries, Esmeray allowed herself to hope, to believe that maybe, just maybe, she didn't have to be alone. That perhaps, love was not a weakness, but a strength, a fire that could melt the ice around her heart and allow her to live fully, unafraid.

As they stood together, their arms wrapped around each other, Esmeray felt a sense of peace settle over her, a quiet assurance that love could be something beautiful, something worth fighting for. And as she looked up at Darian, her heart full and open for the first time in centuries, she knew that no matter what challenges lay ahead, she would face them with him by her side.

A Dragon's Choice

The heavy silence between Esmeray and Darian seemed to echo through the castle's great hall. Evening had fallen, casting long shadows over the stone floors and filling the space with a quiet, somber glow. Esmeray stood near one of the large arched windows, her arms crossed as she looked out at the snowy landscape stretching below. She had spent her life as a queen, bound to this kingdom and its cold, unyielding landscape. But now, a new warmth had taken root in her heart, and she didn't know how to reconcile it with the person she had always been.

Darian watched her from the doorway, his expression a mixture of resolve and concern. He knew something was weighing heavily on her, something more than her usual reluctance to let herself feel. After a long pause, he took a deep breath and walked toward her, his footsteps soft but purposeful. She turned slightly as he approached, her gaze guarded but softened by a hint of vulnerability.

"Esmeray," he began, his voice gentle yet firm, "you've been distant since last night. I know there's something you're holding back, something more than the walls you've kept around your heart. You don't have to do this alone."

She hesitated, her gaze flickering between him and the frosty landscape beyond the window. Her heart felt as if it were tearing in two, caught between her duty and the longing that had blossomed within her, a longing she hadn't felt in centuries.

"Darian," she said softly, her voice barely a whisper, "you don't understand what's at stake."

"Then help me understand," he replied, his tone steady as he took another step closer, closing the space between them. "You're afraid, I get that. But this isn't just about your past or the pain you've been through. There's something more, something you're not telling me."

She looked down, her fingers clutching the fabric of her gown as though she could hold herself together through sheer force of will. "I've already told you about the curse," she began, her voice wavering. "That my heart was frozen by magic, that I was cursed to live as a dragon by day and as a queen by night."

Darian nodded, his gaze unwavering. "But that's not the whole truth, is it?"

She took a deep, shaky breath, her gaze hardening as she forced herself to meet his eyes. "There's a price, Darian. If I allow myself to truly feel again, if I let myself fall in love…" She hesitated, the words catching in her throat. "I risk losing everything."

"What do you mean?" he asked, his brow furrowing with concern.

"If I love, Darian, if I let myself be vulnerable again, I risk my power," she explained, her voice thick with emotion. "The magic that binds me to this kingdom, the power that protects these lands… it's tied to my heart, to the ice that surrounds it. If I melt that ice, if I allow my heart to be whole again, I may lose my ability to rule."

He stared at her, absorbing the weight of her words. "You mean… if you choose to love, you could lose your powers? Your kingdom?"

She nodded, her expression filled with anguish. "Yes. I could lose everything I've spent centuries protecting."

Darian took a deep breath, his expression serious. "But, Esmeray… if that's true, then what have you really been protecting? This kingdom is strong, yes, but it's frozen in time, just like you've been. What good is all that power if it keeps you trapped, alone, and in pain?"

Her gaze hardened, a flash of anger flaring in her eyes. "You think I want this?" she demanded, her voice sharp. "You think I enjoy being alone, carrying this burden without anyone to share it with? This curse… it was the price I paid to keep my people safe, to protect them from those who would take everything from us. Alaric stole my heart, my trust, and left me with nothing but this icy prison. I have no choice, Darian."

"Maybe you did once," he replied softly, refusing to back down. "But you have a choice now, Esmeray. You're not the woman you were when you first took on this curse. You're stronger, wiser. And maybe… maybe it's time to think about what you truly want."

She looked at him, a mixture of fear and frustration in her eyes. "And what if what I want means risking everything? My power, my people, this kingdom… they're all bound to me. If I lose my magic, if I lose my ability to rule, then who am I?"

He reached out, his hand resting gently on her arm, grounding her with his warmth. "You're Esmeray. A woman who deserves happiness, who deserves love. And if you choose to trust me, to let me stand beside you… maybe, just maybe, you can have both. You don't have to be alone anymore."

She closed her eyes, feeling the warmth of his hand, the steadiness of his presence, the strength in his words. She wanted to believe him, wanted to trust that love didn't have to mean weakness, that it could be something powerful, something worth fighting for. But the fear remained, an insistent whisper that told her she would lose herself, that she would be left vulnerable and broken once more.

"Darian," she murmured, her voice thick with emotion, "I want to believe you. But if I choose love, if I choose you… I could lose my magic, my strength. I could become powerless."

He moved closer, his other hand gently cupping her face, his thumb brushing over her cheek as he looked into her eyes, his gaze filled with quiet determination. "Then we'll face it together. Love isn't about giving up power—it's about sharing it. It's about having someone by your side, someone who will fight for you, stand with you, no matter what."

A tear slipped down her cheek, and she bit her lip, her heart a storm of conflicting emotions. "But what if it's not enough? What if I lose my power and… and I lose you too?"

He pulled her into his arms, his embrace strong and unwavering, grounding her in a way that made her feel both vulnerable and safe. "I'm not going anywhere, Esmeray," he whispered, his voice filled with quiet conviction. "Whatever happens, whatever choice you make, I'll be here. But I don't want to see you live in fear. You deserve to be free, to feel, to love."

She buried her face in his chest, her hands clutching his shirt as she let herself melt into his embrace, the ice around her heart slowly thawing. She felt the strength in his arms, the steady beat of his heart, a silent promise that he would be there, that he would stand by her, no matter the cost.

For a long moment, they stood together, wrapped in each other's warmth, the weight of her choice settling over them. She pulled back slightly, her gaze meeting his, her eyes filled with both fear and hope.

"If I choose you," she whispered, her voice trembling, "if I choose to love… I may never be able to rule again. I may lose everything I've built, everything I've fought for."

He smiled, his hand gently brushing a strand of hair from her face. "Then let's build something new together. We don't have to follow the path that was set for you, Esmeray. We can create our own, one that's filled with love, with strength. One where you don't have to be alone."

She looked into his eyes, the warmth in his gaze melting the last of her resistance, and for the first time, she allowed herself to believe that maybe, just maybe, love could be something worth risking everything for.

"Then I choose you," she whispered, her voice filled with quiet determination. "I choose love, even if it means giving up my power, my kingdom. I choose a life with you."

He pulled her into a deep, passionate kiss, their embrace filled with a fierce, unspoken promise. She felt herself surrender completely, her heart free and open for the first time in centuries. And as they held each other, the warmth between them a fire that melted the last of the ice around her heart, Esmeray knew she had finally made the right choice.

She was free—free to love, to feel, to live. And no matter what lay ahead, she knew that she would face it with Darian by her side, her heart no longer bound by fear or ice, but by a love that was fierce, unbreakable, and true.

A Love Tested by Fire

The air was thick with tension in the days following Esmeray's decision to embrace her love for Darian. Though they had shared tender moments and promises, a shadow lingered over the castle. Esmeray could feel her powers wane, her magic more difficult to summon with each passing day. Every time she reached for the strength that had once come so easily, it felt elusive, as if her own heart were slipping further from her grasp.

Darian noticed the change, too, though he didn't voice his concerns. Instead, he stayed by her side, steadfast and unwavering, offering her the quiet support she needed, even as he saw the worry in her eyes.

One evening, as they walked along the ramparts of the castle, he broke the silence. "I know you're struggling, Esmeray. I can feel it. You don't have to hide it from me."

She glanced away, her gaze fixed on the horizon where the sky was painted in shades of red and violet as the sun dipped below the mountains. "I'm afraid, Darian," she admitted, her voice barely audible. "I can feel my magic slipping. It's like… part of me is fading."

He reached for her hand, entwining his fingers with hers, his touch grounding. "Then let me carry that fear with you," he said softly. "You've spent so long fighting alone. You don't have to anymore."

A faint smile touched her lips as she turned to him, her eyes softening. "You are relentless, you know that?"

"Only when it comes to you," he replied, a hint of a smile playing on his lips. He leaned down, pressing a gentle kiss to her forehead, his voice dropping to a tender whisper. "You're worth every risk, every fight."

She looked up at him, her heart swelling with love and fear in equal measure. "Darian, if it comes to it… if I lose everything… promise me you'll be all right. I don't want you to sacrifice yourself for me."

He held her gaze, his expression serious. "Esmeray, I'm not going anywhere. Whatever comes, we face it together."

Before she could reply, a distant roar shattered the quiet, and she felt her heart lurch as a flicker of fiery light lit up the horizon. Shadows moved over the mountains, and she recognized the shape of dragons—rival dragons—drawing closer, their wings spread wide against the darkening sky.

"They're coming," she whispered, dread pooling in her stomach. "They've sensed my weakness. They know I'm vulnerable."

Darian's grip on her hand tightened. "Then we'll show them that we're stronger together."

They hurried to the main courtyard, where soldiers and guards were already preparing for battle, their faces tense with fear and determination. Thorian met them near the gates, his expression grim as he took in the approaching dragons.

"They've gathered all their forces," he said, his voice laced with worry. "They're planning a final assault. If they break through the gates…"

Esmeray's gaze hardened as she looked out at the approaching enemy. "Then we'll make sure they don't."

She transformed into her dragon form, her scales shimmering with an ethereal light, though she could feel the strain on her magic, the weight of her waning power. Darian watched her, his face filled with a mix of awe and concern as he took in the fierce beauty of her dragon form.

Without hesitation, he drew his sword, standing by her side as she spread her wings, ready to defend the kingdom and the love they had only just begun to build.

The first wave of dragons descended upon them, their roars echoing through the night as they unleashed streams of fire toward the castle. Esmeray took to the sky, her movements powerful but slightly slower than usual, the toll of her weakening magic evident in the strain of her wings.

Darian fought on the ground, his sword flashing as he cut through the ranks of rival warriors who had joined the dragons, his movements swift and deadly. He was relentless, every strike filled with the fierce determination to protect the woman he loved, even as he saw her struggling in the air above.

Esmeray faced off against a particularly large dragon, its scales dark as night, its eyes filled with malice as it lunged at her. She twisted, barely dodging its attack, and retaliated with a blast of icy breath that momentarily stunned her opponent. But her magic faltered, the ice weaker than it should have been, and she felt a surge of panic as the dragon recovered, lunging toward her with renewed ferocity.

Below, Darian saw her stumble in the air, his heart racing as he realized the depth of her struggle. He shouted up to her, his voice filled with both desperation and encouragement. "Esmeray! You're stronger than this! Don't let them take that from you!"

His words bolstered her, and with a fierce roar, she summoned the last reserves of her strength, slashing at the rival dragon with her claws, driving it back. But she knew she couldn't hold out forever. The strain of the battle was taking its toll, her magic slipping further away with each passing moment.

Just as she thought she couldn't hold on any longer, Darian climbed a nearby turret, calling out to her again. "Esmeray! Look at me!"

She turned, her dragon eyes locking onto his, and in that moment, she felt his unwavering support, his love surrounding her like a shield. Her heart surged with warmth, the ice within her melting as she drew strength from his gaze.

A rival dragon dove toward Darian, its jaws open, fire gleaming in its throat, and without a second thought, she lunged, intercepting the creature mid-air. She fought with everything she had, her movements fueled not by magic but by sheer will, by the need to protect the man who had shown her that love was not a weakness.

With one final, powerful strike, she defeated the dragon, sending it plummeting to the ground. But as she landed beside Darian, her strength gave out, and she stumbled, her dragon form flickering as she struggled to maintain it.

Darian rushed to her side, his hands reaching out to steady her as she transformed back into her human form, her body weakened, her breath ragged. "Esmeray," he murmured, his voice filled with worry as he held her close. "Are you all right?"

She looked up at him, her eyes filled with both fear and determination. "I... I don't know how much longer I can hold onto my powers, Darian. They're slipping away."

He cupped her face, his gaze filled with fierce resolve. "Then let them go. You don't need them to be strong. You don't need magic to be a queen."

Tears filled her eyes as she looked at him, her heart breaking at the thought of losing everything she had known, everything she had fought to protect. "But if I lose my powers... I lose part of who I am."

He leaned down, pressing his forehead against hers, his voice a soft murmur. "Your power isn't what makes you a queen, Esmeray. It's your heart, your courage, your love for your people. That's what makes you strong."

She closed her eyes, his words washing over her, filling her with a newfound strength that went beyond magic, beyond power. She took a deep, steadying breath, the last of her fear melting away as she accepted the truth he had shown her.

When she opened her eyes, the love she felt for him was clear, a quiet, fierce resolve that radiated from her. "Then I will fight, Darian. I will fight with everything I have, even if that means fighting without magic."

He smiled, his hands still cradling her face as he pressed a gentle kiss to her forehead. "That's all I ask."

Together, they turned to face the final wave of enemies, their hearts intertwined, their love a powerful force that transcended magic. Though Esmeray could feel her powers slipping, she fought with a strength she hadn't known she possessed, each strike, each movement filled with a fierce determination to protect the kingdom and the man she loved.

As dawn broke over the horizon, the last of the rival dragons retreated, their forces scattered. The castle was battered, the land scarred, but they had won. Esmeray stood beside Darian, her heart pounding with both relief and a quiet joy as she looked out over the battlefield.

She reached for his hand, her voice a soft whisper. "We did it."

He looked down at her, his gaze filled with pride and love. "You did it, Esmeray. You fought with everything you had, and you proved that your strength goes beyond magic."

She smiled, leaning into him as he wrapped his arms around her, holding her close. For the first time, she felt truly free, no longer bound by the curse that had defined her life. And as she looked up at him, her heart full of love and hope, she knew that whatever lay ahead, she would face it with him by her side.

The Betrayal Revealed

The battlefield was quiet now, the sun casting a soft golden glow over the battered landscape. The dawn after the battle felt surreal; the castle grounds, once filled with the thunderous roars of dragons and the clash of swords, were now eerily silent. Esmeray walked through the ruins with Darian by her side, her hand tightly held in his, both of them exhausted yet victorious. She could feel her heart finally settling, a warmth growing inside her that she hadn't felt in centuries—a warmth she now knew was from a love that had stood the test of fire and battle.

But as they neared the castle's main hall, a noise caught Darian's attention. He squeezed her hand and pulled her slightly behind him, his gaze sharpening as he drew his sword. "Stay back, Esmeray," he murmured, his tone firm.

"What is it?" she asked, worry flickering in her eyes as she watched him move forward, his body tense and ready.

A figure stepped out from the shadows near the grand staircase, a man clad in dark leather armor with a wicked glint in his eyes. Darian's grip on his sword tightened as he recognized the man—a dragon slayer, marked by the scar on his cheek and the emblem on his chest. Esmeray's eyes widened as she, too, recognized the figure from stories of the past.

"Eldric," she breathed, her voice laced with both anger and confusion.

Eldric smirked, his gaze flickering over her with disdain. "So, the Ice Queen is alive after all," he sneered. "And here I thought I'd find you frozen in some dark tower, wallowing in your curse."

Darian stepped forward, his sword pointed at Eldric's chest. "You have no place here," he growled. "Your kind has already done enough damage."

Eldric chuckled, unfazed. "Oh, you're wrong, my friend. My kind has only just begun. You see, it was I who helped Alaric all those years ago. We both saw the potential in Esmeray's power, the way it could be harnessed, controlled. A pity Alaric was such a fool, leaving me to finish what he couldn't."

Esmeray felt the blood drain from her face as she realized the truth. Her curse, her centuries of loneliness and heartache, had not been some twisted punishment from the gods. It had been orchestrated by the man who now stood before her, the same man who had plotted with Alaric, the love she had once trusted.

"Why?" she whispered, her voice trembling with a mixture of fury and heartbreak. "Why would you do this to me? To my kingdom?"

Eldric shrugged, his gaze cold and calculating. "Power, of course. Your magic was extraordinary, Esmeray. But you were weak, blinded by love. Alaric knew that if we couldn't have your magic, then we would at least ensure that you would never use it freely. The curse? It was a brilliant strategy. Your heart encased in ice, your powers bound to your emotions. As long as you remained afraid, your magic would be ours to control, to manipulate as we saw fit."

Her hands trembled, the weight of his words crashing over her like a tidal wave. She had spent centuries in isolation, fearing her own heart, believing that love had cursed her, when in reality, it was nothing but a lie, a manipulation.

Darian moved closer, his eyes blazing with anger. "You stole her life for the sake of your greed? You made her suffer for centuries, and for what? Power you never even managed to claim?"

Eldric laughed, his tone mocking. "Love is nothing but weakness, boy. I did what had to be done. Esmeray was too powerful to be left unchecked. And look at her now—she's broken, her magic weakened, all because she let herself love again."

Esmeray's fists clenched, her sorrow giving way to a fierce, burning rage that simmered in her veins. She took a step forward, her voice cold yet filled with fire. "You may have taken my past from me, Eldric, but you will not have my future. I am no longer the frightened woman you cursed. I have found my strength, a strength that has nothing to do with you or your twisted schemes."

Eldric sneered, drawing a blade from his belt, its steel glinting dangerously in the light. "We'll see about that, Ice Queen."

Without hesitation, Darian stepped in front of her, his sword raised. "You'll have to go through me first," he said, his tone deadly calm.

Eldric lunged forward, his blade aimed at Darian's chest, but Darian blocked the strike, their swords clashing with a metallic ring that echoed through the hall. The two men circled each other, their movements sharp and calculated, each strike filled with a lethal precision. Esmeray watched, her heart pounding, every instinct screaming at her to fight, to protect Darian as he protected her.

As they fought, Eldric taunted Darian, his words filled with malice. "You think you can protect her? You're just another pawn, another fool who will be discarded once she's done with you. Just like Alaric."

Darian's jaw tightened, his gaze filled with fierce resolve. "You don't know anything about her," he spat, deflecting another blow and pressing forward, his movements fueled by his love for Esmeray, by the promise he had made to stand by her side.

Eldric laughed, his voice cold and bitter. "Oh, but I know everything about her. I know her fears, her weaknesses. I made her."

"No," Esmeray interjected, stepping forward, her voice filled with a steely resolve that surprised even herself. "You didn't make me. You tried to break me, but I am still here, stronger than ever. And I am not alone."

In that moment, something shifted within her, a warmth that filled her heart, melting the last remnants of ice that had bound her for so long. She felt her magic surge, but it was different now, less bound by fear and more connected to the love she had embraced, the love that made her stronger, not weaker.

As Darian and Eldric continued to clash, Esmeray took a deep breath, feeling the warmth of her magic spread through her veins. She raised her hand, and with a focused surge of power, she summoned an icy wind that wrapped around Eldric, freezing his movements. He struggled, but her magic held him in place, her gaze hard and unyielding as she approached him.

"You took my past," she said, her voice steady and filled with a quiet strength, "but you will not take my future."

With one final surge of power, she encased him in a thick layer of ice, freezing him in place. Eldric's face twisted in fury, but he was helpless against her magic, his fate sealed.

Darian sheathed his sword, turning to her with a mixture of awe and pride in his eyes. "Esmeray… you did it."

She looked at him, her gaze softening, the rage and sorrow replaced by a quiet peace. "No, Darian," she whispered, taking his hand, her fingers intertwining with his. "We did it. Together."

He pulled her into his arms, his embrace warm and comforting as he held her close. "Are you all right?" he murmured, his voice filled with concern as he gently brushed a strand of hair from her face.

She nodded, a tear slipping down her cheek, though this one was filled with relief, with joy. "For the first time in centuries… I am."

They stood there in silence, wrapped in each other's arms, their hearts beating in sync, bound not by fear or manipulation, but by a love that had endured every trial, every test. And as they held each other, Esmeray felt the weight of her past lift, replaced by a newfound strength, a freedom that came from embracing not only her magic but her heart.

Darian's eyes softened as he met her gaze, his hand gently tracing the line of her jaw, his thumb brushing against her cheek. He leaned down, his forehead resting against hers, their breaths mingling as he whispered, "You're free now, Esmeray. Free to live, to love… to be everything you were meant to be."

Her heart swelled with emotion, and without hesitation, she closed the distance between them, capturing his lips in a kiss filled with all the passion, all the love, she had held back for so long. The world seemed to fade around them as she poured everything into that kiss, her hands tangling in his hair, her body pressed close to his as if she never wanted to let him go.

Darian responded in kind, his arms wrapping around her, pulling her even closer as his lips moved against hers with a fierce, unyielding tenderness. The kiss was filled with unspoken promises, a declaration of love that went beyond words, beyond time. She could feel the warmth of his touch spreading through her, melting the last remnants of ice that had once guarded her heart.

As they finally pulled back, both breathless, Darian's eyes were filled with a gentle intensity as he looked down at her, his hand still cradling her face. "Esmeray," he murmured, his voice filled with awe, "I love you. More than anything."

A tear slipped down her cheek, but this time it was a tear of joy, of release. She smiled, her voice soft yet steady. "And I love you, Darian. You've given me back my life, my heart. You've made me believe in love again."

They shared another kiss, slower this time, savoring the moment, the certainty that they had finally found each other against all odds. And as they stood together in the soft light of dawn, Esmeray knew that she had not only reclaimed her kingdom, her freedom, but had found a love that would carry her through whatever lay ahead—a love that was as fierce, as eternal as the magic that bound their souls together.

Hearts of Ice, Hearts of Fire

The castle was aglow with soft candlelight, casting warm, flickering shadows across the stone walls. It was as if the entire kingdom were celebrating, each corner of the castle filled with fresh flowers, laughter, and the lingering scent of rich spices from the wedding feast. But now, as night had fallen and the celebration had wound down, it was quiet, and Esmeray could hear only the gentle crackle of the fire in the hearth.

She stood near the window in her bedchamber, her fingers nervously tracing the intricate lace of her wedding gown. Though her icy powers had faded, she felt more powerful, more alive, than she ever had before. It was as if every touch, every breath, was heightened, vibrant, carrying with it a warmth she had never imagined.

Behind her, the door opened with a soft creak, and she felt her heart flutter as Darian stepped into the room. She turned, a smile spreading across her face as she met his gaze. He looked at her with a quiet reverence, his eyes filled with a tenderness that made her knees go weak.

"You're breathtaking," he murmured, crossing the room toward her, his gaze never leaving her face. He wore a simple but elegant tunic, his hair still tousled from the festivities, and he looked both regal and relaxed, a warmth in his eyes that left her breathless.

Esmeray blushed, her smile turning shy as she looked down. "Thank you," she whispered. "Tonight feels like a dream."

Darian reached out, gently lifting her chin with his fingers, his touch light but full of intention. "Then let's never wake up," he murmured, his voice a soft promise that made her heart race.

He leaned down, capturing her lips in a kiss that was both gentle and passionate, a kiss that seemed to melt away the last remnants of her fear and hesitation. She melted against him, her hands resting on his chest as she felt his heart beating beneath her fingertips, steady and strong.

Their kiss deepened, slow and unhurried, as if they had all the time in the world. His hands slid to her waist, pulling her close, and she responded with equal fervor, her arms wrapping around his neck as she pressed herself against him. The warmth of his body, the feel of his lips on hers, was intoxicating, and she felt as if she were floating, lost in the heat of their embrace.

He pulled back just slightly, his forehead resting against hers as they caught their breath, his fingers tracing gentle patterns along her back. "Esmeray," he whispered, his voice filled with a love that made her heart swell. "Tonight is ours. Nothing else matters—only us."

She looked up at him, her eyes filled with both excitement and a lingering nervousness. "I've waited so long for this," she murmured, her voice barely a whisper. "To be with someone who loves me… not for my power, not for what I can give, but for me."

Darian's expression softened, his gaze filled with a fierce devotion as he cupped her face in his hands. "Esmeray, I love you for who you are, every part of you—your strength, your kindness, the fire in your heart. I would follow you to the ends of the earth. I am yours, now and always."

A tear slipped down her cheek, and he brushed it away with his thumb, his touch tender as he kissed her again, his lips soft and warm against hers. This kiss was different—deeper, more passionate, as if he were pouring all his love, his promises, into that one touch. She felt her own heart respond, her hands tightening around him as she let herself fall completely, surrendering to the moment, to him.

His hands slid down her arms, taking her hands in his as he led her toward the bed, his gaze never leaving hers. They stood at the edge, his fingers gently caressing her skin as he looked at her with a mixture of love and desire that made her heart race. "Are you sure?" he asked softly, his voice filled with reverence.

She nodded, her voice steady as she looked up at him. "I've never been more certain of anything in my life."

With that, he lifted her hand to his lips, pressing a soft kiss to her palm before leaning down to capture her lips once more. Their movements were slow, unhurried, each touch, each kiss filled with a tender passion that left them both breathless. His hands traced the curves of her body, each touch igniting a fire within her that left her aching for more.

Her fingers found their way to the clasps of his tunic, her hands shaking slightly as she undid them, her gaze meeting his as she worked. He watched her, his eyes dark with love and desire, his breath hitching as her hands brushed against his skin. When his tunic slipped to the floor, she took a moment to admire him, her eyes tracing the lines of his chest, her heart pounding as she took in the sight of him.

"You're beautiful," she whispered, her voice filled with awe as she reached out, her fingers grazing his skin.

He smiled, his hands moving to her waist as he pulled her close, his lips finding hers in another kiss, this one filled with a growing intensity that left her breathless. She felt her heart racing, the warmth between them building as they slowly undressed, each touch, each kiss filled with the promise of a love that would endure.

When they finally lay together, wrapped in each other's arms, their bodies pressed close, Esmeray felt as though she had found her home. Every touch, every kiss, was a silent vow, a promise of forever, and she felt her heart swell with a love that was as fierce as it was tender.

Darian's hands traced gentle patterns along her skin, his lips pressing soft kisses along her shoulder, her neck, each touch filled with reverence, with devotion. She felt as though she were melting, her entire being consumed by the warmth of his love, by the fire that burned between them.

"Esmeray," he murmured, his voice filled with wonder as he looked into her eyes. "You're everything I've ever wanted, everything I never knew I needed. I love you, with all that I am."

She smiled, her fingers brushing through his hair as she looked up at him, her own gaze filled with love. "And I love you, Darian. You've given me a life I never dreamed possible. You've made me feel alive."

Their lips met in another kiss, slow and deep, each movement filled with a love that seemed to go beyond words, beyond time. They held each other close, their hearts beating in perfect harmony, their bodies and souls entwined as one.

As the night wore on, they lay together, sharing soft whispers, gentle laughter, their love filling the room like a warm, comforting glow. They spoke of their future, of the life they would build together, of the dreams they would share. And as the first light of dawn crept over the horizon, casting a soft glow over the room, they knew that they were no longer bound by fear or doubt.

They were bound by love, by a fire that would never fade, a fire that would carry them through whatever lay ahead. And as they lay in each other's arms, Esmeray felt her heart swell with a quiet, unbreakable joy, a joy that she knew would last forever.

For they were no longer hearts of ice and fire. They were one—bound together by a love that would endure for all time.